CW01011227

WOF

Poetry

Thirteen Ways of Looking at the Highlands
(Diehard Publishers, 1996)
Seven Senses (Diehard Publishers, 2000)
Mementoliths (Calder Wood Press, 2005)
Sushi & Chips (Diehard Publishers, 2006)
The floor show at the Mad Yak Café (Red Squirrel Press, 2010)
The Propriety of Weeding (Red Squirrel Press, 2012)
The Year's Six Seasons (Calder Wood Press, 2013)
The Book of Ways (Red Squirrel Press, 2014)
The Night I Danced With Maya (Red Squirrel Press, 2017)

Short Stories

Getting On (Postbox Press, 2016)

Word Play

Short Stories

Colin Will

Postbox
PRESS

First published in 2018 by Postbox Press,
the literary fiction imprint of Red Squirrel Press
36 Elphinstone Crescent
Biggar
South Lanarkshire
ML12 6GU
www.redsquirrelpress.com

Typesetting and design by Gerry Cambridge
e: gerry.cambridge@btinternet.com

A CIP catalogue record for this book is available from the
British Library.

ISBN: 978 1 910437 48 3

Red Squirrel Press/Postbox Press are committed to a sustainable
future. This book is printed in the UK by Imprint Digital using
Forest Stewardship Council certified paper.

~ Contents ~

~ Word Play ~

THE FIRST SIX MONTHS were the worst. After that, the second six months were the worst. What I'm trying to say is that there was no single moment in that first year when I thought, *I'm beginning to get over it*. Because I don't really think I will ever get over it. But there are moments, minutes, hours maybe, when I don't think about Sandra.

When a partner dies, at some stage you say goodbye to your grief, and you learn to adjust, to get by, to continue living singly, rather than as a couple. But when your partner falls obsessively in love with someone else and goes off, leaving you and your shared children behind, the grief is open-ended, the adjustment incomplete. You can't just move on.

Sandra's parents were great with our two, Liam and Katy. Maybe some of it was guilt for what their daughter had done to our family, but they were wonderful, especially in those first fraught weeks. They saw the children most weekends, and they found a local childminder for me, a very nice woman who picked up the kids from school and took them home with her until I finished work and collected them from her. Linda was a single mum, bringing up two of her own children, and my two liked her, and got on well with her children. She offered to make their evening meals for Liam and Katy, but I insisted on doing that when we got home. It made me feel fatherly, the provider, apart from the night I burned the mince. I will never forget the smell of burning mince. But we were still a family.

Liam was thirteen, two years older than Katy, and was always closer to his mother, so he felt her loss very deeply.

He was quiet, thoughtful, but not withdrawn. I asked him to help Katy with her homework, and he was very patient. He had a few close friends at school, but no real friends near where we lived. Katy had always been outgoing, full of energy and with a lively mind. She seemed to adjust more quickly, although sometimes the tears did come when I tucked her up in bed. I love my children so fiercely that it surprises me sometimes. We didn't talk about Mum very often, but I always made sure I never said anything against her, nor her decision to leave us. Of course, some nights my pillow was as wet as Katy's, but I don't think the kids ever heard me crying.

I blame Tom Stoppard for the whole mess. Well, that's not true; it was all Sandra and Oliver's doing, but it was when they were acting together in one of his plays—*The Real Thing*—that it all started. It's a confusing but beautifully written play, with many of Stoppard's hallmark devices—play within a play, confusion between reality and theatre, and great inventive wit. Sandra played Annie, the mistress of a playwright, and Oliver played Billy, a young actor smitten by Annie, his co-actor in *'Tis Pity She's A Whore*, the play within the play within the play. Cunning fellow, Stoppard. In the play, both swear it's an emotional affair, not a physical one, but Annie refuses to give Billy up. Babysitting duties meant that I missed the performances, but friends said Sandra was extremely good in it. I could believe it; she's always been good on stage. At the end of the run Sandra said she'd be going to the after-show party, and that she'd be home late.

I have no idea what time it was when she did get home, but after-show parties were always late-night affairs, and I'd never worried about her in the past. I woke up and started making the kids' breakfasts, letting her sleep on. She was really out of it. I looked out of the front window and couldn't see Sandra's Mini. She must have had too much to drink, and taken a taxi home. The responsible adult in me was happy that she'd done the sensible thing. After she'd risen and had her own breakfast the four of us drove over to where she thought she'd parked her car. It was in a part of town neither of us knew. The children thought it was a great adventure, *Helping Mummy Find Her Car*, and it was pretty funny. I was in a good mood, teasing Sandra about how much she'd had to drink at the party. She ignored me, face screwed up with concern until she spotted the car.

'Oh, good, it's still in one piece,' she said.

'Who is it you know that lives round here?' I asked.

'Ollie, Oliver,' she replied.

I seemed to remember being told the party would be at Christine's flat, the woman who'd played the other female lead, but I didn't say anything. Sandra jumped into her car and drove off, arriving home just before us.

Twice during the following week Sandra phoned me at work, asking me to look after Liam and Katy while she went out with friends. On both occasions she came home around 11, but I didn't think she'd been drinking.

The next week followed the same pattern. Monday and Wednesday she was out with friends, while I looked after our children. On the Friday morning she told me she was going out again that night, and not to wait up for her.

I woke up on the Saturday morning, alone in bed. Her side of the bed hadn't been slept in. I was really alarmed, and I ran downstairs, naked, to phone the police. Sandra was sitting quietly in the living room.

'When did you get home?' I asked.

'About half an hour ago.'

'What do you mean?'

'I stayed with Ollie last night. We're in love. I'm moving in with him.'

She spoke quite calmly, as if she'd said she was just going to the shops for milk and bread. A lot of things fell into place then.

'I came back to get some things. I'll come back for the rest another time. You're not going to make a scene, are you?'

'No, it looks like it's gone beyond that.' I said. I went upstairs and dressed, coming back down to make the children their breakfasts. I've always liked doing that for them, giving them a good start to the day, even when my day was fubar. The routine didn't really help take my mind off what she'd said. Sandra bustled about, bringing a couple of empty suitcases in from the garage, and filling them with her clothes and toiletries. I guessed she'd need a few more journeys—Minis don't hold that much.

'When can we talk?' I asked.

'I'll come back tomorrow. I'll phone my parents and ask them to take the children for the day.'

'Right. Well. Goodbye then.'

'Goodbye Ade. I'll see you tomorrow.' And she was off.

It was terribly hard to pretend in front of the children that everything was normal, when they both knew it wasn't. Sandra's father phoned me.

'Morning Adrian. Sandra's just told us. I'm shocked, and very disappointed in her. I can't believe she'd do this. I just want you to know that Molly and I love you and our grandchildren. We'll do whatever we can for you.'

'Thank you James. That means a lot to me.'

'You've always been good to her. How could she...?' and he started crying, which set me off too. We hung up.

I got through the day somehow, taking the kids to play in the park, meeting a couple of neighbours, coming home to make a light lunch, taking Katy round to her friend's house, helping Liam with his homework, then cooking supper, a bit of mindless TV, getting first Katy then Liam bathed and off to bed. Then I could sit down by myself and let myself go. All cried out, I was in bed by 10, but I couldn't sleep.

James came over next morning to take Liam and Katy away. His eyes were red too. Then, late morning, Sandra came back with her empty suitcases.

'Can we talk?'

'Yes. We have to,' I said. During that long restless night I had eventually made up my mind about what to say.

'I'm sorry Adrian. I didn't mean this to happen.'

'But it did.'

'Yes. It came totally out of the blue, completely unexpected. I wasn't looking for anything to happen, but when Ollie and I were on stage together it just ... did. We looked at each other in that scene, and I knew I wanted him. We were all over each other afterwards, and then at the after-show party we left early and went over to his place. It was explosive. I couldn't get enough of him, and I still can't. I'm sorry, but I need to tell somebody—anybody— how it was. I'm sorry if it hurts you.'

'It does.'

'And then I went to him twice the next week, and three times last week. I slept with him on Friday night, and again last night. I'm going to live with him.'

'For how long?' I asked.

'This isn't just a casual fling, Adrian. I love him. He loves me. We belong together.'

'That's very clear then. I've thought about it overnight and this morning, and this is what I'm suggesting. On Monday I'll see a lawyer and start divorce proceedings. Adultery makes things much quicker. It could be almost immediate, as soon as we can get a hearing. You'll admit to adultery?'

'Of course. I could hardly deny it.'

'I want custody of Liam and Katy, but you can visit them as often as you want, as long we arrange it beforehand. No overnight visits though, and no holiday visits.'

'I can agree to that. Overnighters would be impossible in Ollie's wee flat.'

'And Oliver never enters this house. I won't allow that Sandra.' She nodded.

'Now, money and property. The house was left to me by my parents before we married, so that's not part of the settlement. You have no rights over it, especially if the children are staying here.'

'Are you sure?'

'Definitely. I've checked what the law says.'

'I'll have to take your word for that.'

'No need. The lawyers will confirm. Now, I earn maybe a third more than you, but I'll have the children to look after, so I think it would be fair just to suggest there will be no element of support on either side. Do you agree?'

'Yes, that seems fair. There don't seem any prospects of promotion in the library, but we'll get by with Ollie's salary and mine.'

'Are there any bits of furniture you want? We probably bought most of it together.'

'I can't think of anything. You'll need most of it for you and the children anyway.'

'Then I think that's everything. I'll draw up the terms with the lawyer tomorrow and he'll send them to you for signature. Let me have a note of your address.'

'Of course.' She paused. 'I didn't know what to expect this morning—a blazing row, a shouting match, tears, but I didn't expect you to have it all worked out like this.'

'Oh, there have been tears, Sandra, and there will be more, no doubt.'

'Right. I'll pack some more clothes and things.'

'Need any help?

'No, I'll manage.' She went upstairs with her suitcases, and I sat in the kitchen with a coffee. When she came downstairs with her cases, I asked her if she thought she'd marry Oliver when our decree came through. She said they hadn't talked that far ahead, but she hoped they would. And then she walked out of my life. Except of course she didn't.

After she left I went round the house, putting her other things into bin bags for her to collect. There wasn't much; some old clothes and shoes I was sure she wouldn't want, some personal knick-knacks I had no use for, a couple of handbags and purses, play scripts, nothing important. I took down most of the photos, apart from the ones with the children in.

On the Monday my lawyer drew up the terms, and sent Sandra an affidavit for signature, admitting adultery with 'a Mr Oliver McKechnie'. I honestly didn't think there might have been others, although I know how intense theatrical relationships can get. The line between performance and real life can get blurred at times. For that reason I never blamed Sandra, although her throwaway remark about 'casual flings' did give me some concerns. But this situation was far more serious. I would probably have been able to come to terms with a casual fling, if she'd had one, if I'd known about it.

I know the world of amateur drama very well, having been involved with it for several years, although not recently. In fact, that was how we met, fifteen years before, shy but excited, on stage together for the first time. It was very sweet.

I closed our joint account and sent her a cheque for half the amount, and I arranged for a locksmith to come in and change our locks. I don't think I was being petty, but I didn't want to take the chance that Oliver might get access to the house by using Sandra's keys. I just didn't trust him.

She phoned twice that first week to arrange visits. We sat round the kitchen table and told the children that Mummy was no longer living with us; she had moved into a new place in the city. We told the children it wasn't their fault that this was happening, they had done nothing wrong. Liam, that very perceptive boy, said, 'I expect your new place is near where you lost your car.' Sandra blushed and nodded. I'm pretty sure that, even at that stage, he had put two and two together.

The early visits, when Sandra came on her own, went well. She took them out; they went to cafes, parks, the Museum, and the Modern Art Gallery. Katy loved art, and she was very enthusiastic. I made a mental note to encourage her interest. The weekend visits, when she brought Oliver round in her car for trips further afield, were much more sticky, although he never tried to come in. After six months she came round one Sunday to take them both for a trip to Queensferry. Katy put her foot down. Oliver was sitting outside in the passenger seat of Sandra's car—he didn't drive—and Katy point-blank said she didn't want to go, she'd rather stay with Daddy. Perhaps Sandra thought I'd intervene, but I didn't.

'All right Katy, you can stay. Let's get you ready then, Liam,' she said.

'Sorry Mum, I've got things to revise for school,' he said.

Sandra stared silently at the pair of them, then at me. I shrugged my shoulders. I hadn't seen this coming, but I couldn't be unhappy about it.

Liam put his arm around Katy. 'Please don't bring that man round again, Mum. We don't like him.' I wanted to hug the pair of them and shout out loud, but I daren't open my mouth. Still saying nothing, Sandra walked out to her car. I could see the pair talking heatedly, perhaps arguing, then she drove off.

She never did bring him round again. She took Liam out to the pictures for his 14th birthday, and he loved it. She got Katy interested in modern dance, and I happily began ferrying her into town for classes. Her visits were maybe twice a week for the first few months, then once a week, and finally once a month, after the divorce was final. The children seemed to be growing up unscarred, and it seemed that between me, our childminder and my in-laws, they never lacked for companionship and love. Sometimes my mother-in-law Molly would come over and stay in the guestroom to let me go to jazz concerts, an interest of mine that Sandra never took to. Sometimes I met up with friends, although many of 'our' friends turned out to be

Sandra's friends. They dropped me right away. I didn't go out with any women for the whole of that first six month period, but I did meet up with a group of my fellow workers for the occasional Friday Happy Hour. To be perfectly frank, I just didn't feel like starting anything new, and I was long since out of the habit of dating.

Things were looking up at work after my most recent Annual Review and I was hopeful of a promotion into First Division territory. In the meantime I was my usual diligent self. One of the odd things was that Oliver worked in the same government Department as I did, but in a different section, and of course he was at a more junior level. Our paths had never actually crossed, work-wise, but if we saw each other in a corridor we studiously avoided meeting each other's eyes. It's funny how one's background doesn't really count for much in the Service. I mean how did a good degree in English and History qualify me to work in Buildings and Procurement? But I liked the work, and I was good at it. My boss, Tom Sanders, called me in to his office.

'Good morning Adrian, I trust you are well?'

'Very well thank you Tom.'

'Good. The reason I've called you in is that I am to be transferred shortly to the Finance Department. That will leave a vacancy as Head of Section. My superiors and I, in consultation with HR, think that you'd be the ideal person for the job.'

'Thank you Tom, I'm flabbergasted, to be truthful.'

'No Adrian, you deserve it. There's just one delicate little matter we have to discuss first.'

'Yes?' I queried.

'Yes, it concerns a member of staff in Contracts. We have reason to believe he's been skimming some of the contracts, perhaps even receiving considerations from some contractors.'

'And this is delicate because...?' I asked.

'Tell me it's none of my business if you like, tell me to shut up, but your ex-wife...'

'It's Oliver McKechnie, isn't it?'

'It is. The evidence we have is circumstantial at the moment, but we'd like him to resign rather than face a full investigation, which could be nasty and prolonged, and might uncover even more than we suspect at this stage.'

'I can imagine.'

'We don't want to put you in charge of the whole Section before we drop the axe. He might construe that as personal vindictiveness, perhaps even force a legal action against the Department. It could become messy.'

'I can see that. So what happens next?'

'Your salary increase and seniority will start immediately, but you won't take up the post until some time after he's left. We think three months should do it. Martin and I are seeing him next week. I'm hoping it will be an offer he can't refuse, to paraphrase a well-known saying. We won't penalise him, and we'll give him a good reference. That's already been written. We just want shot of him.'

'I see.'

'And we want you to work on a stricter compliance regime, so it can't happen again. You can start that right away?'

'I'll do that. Thank you Sir.'

'You'll do well, Adrian. And I'm desperately sorry to hear about...'

'Sandra.'

'Yes of course, Sandra. Thank you Adrian.'

Oliver did resign, and three months later I was in my new post as head of Section, dealing with both Procurement and Contracts for a sizeable part of the Scottish Government's land and buildings. Sandra never mentioned Oliver's resignation when she came to visit the children.

Some time later she phoned me on a Friday evening, wanting to come round to talk to me. She asked if I could make sure the children weren't around. I thought it was a bit mysterious, but I agreed, taking them round to her parents for the evening.

Sandra came in, and I was astonished by her appearance. She was wearing a white fake-fur bolero jacket over a gold-coloured dress which was extremely short. Her shoes were stilettos, very tall and pointed. She had gold bracelets on her wrists, and she was heavily made up. To me she looked very attractive, but then she always did.

'I need to talk to you about Ollie,' she said.

'I'm listening,' I replied cautiously.

'Did you know he'd lost his job?'

'I heard he'd resigned.'

'He says he was sacked. Did you know anything about it?'

'I didn't at the time, but I've heard a bit since.'

'What have you heard?'

'Well, there were... financial irregularities in some of his contracts, and there were suspicions over his closeness to some contractors. He was asked to resign rather than face a full enquiry, and he did. I must say again that Contracts wasn't part of my remit at the time. I wasn't involved. I mostly worked with architects and surveyors, the technical side of things.'

'I'll tell him. He thinks you were behind it.'

'Tell him I wasn't—I couldn't have been. That's not how the Service works. I was asked to tighten up procedures in Contracts, but that was long after he left. I did hear he was given good references.'

'They haven't done him much good so far. He's still unemployed. I think word got around after he left the Civil Service.'

'That's unfortunate.'

'Very. Most of the time he sits at home, filling in job applications and sending in his CV. It doesn't help with the rent on the flat though. It's been down to me to try to earn more.'

'How have you been doing that?' I asked.

'I tried waitressing and bar work in the evenings, on top of my library job, but they were all minimum wage affairs, or under the counter work for even less.'

'So what did you do?'

'One of my girlfriends suggested escort work. I thought about it for a long time, until things got really bad, then I signed up with an escort agency. I do three nights a week, Friday, Saturday, Sunday. The money's great. I get 40% of the agency fee, and any tips I get I can keep. Of course, I have to do things to earn the tips, but I usually don't mind that. Sometimes the sex is great. And I have a lot of regular clients who like the more mature woman. I told Ollie that I got a job as a cocktail bar waitress at weekends, but I think he suspects the truth. He never says anything, but he doesn't have much choice in the matter, not if he wants to keep a roof over our heads.'

'And do you still…?

'I still love him Adrian. Although I have regrets at times.'

'And he still loves you?'

'Yes, but maybe things have cooled down a bit for him, especially recently.'

'So what brings you here tonight?'

'Apart from the heart-to-heart about Ollie, you mean?' I nodded. 'I have a client that I'm meeting nearby in North Berwick, so I thought I'd pop in. He's an American, over to play golf. He wants a dinner companion to flirt with, a few drinks, a few dances, some energetic sex in his hotel room. He'll go home with happy memories of Scottish hospitality, and I'll go home well fed and a lot richer.'

'Not the way I imagined things turning out, Sandra.'

'I don't know Ade. You know what they say about actresses and whores? Anyway, I must go. Believe it, or don't believe it, but I enjoyed seeing you tonight.'

'Thank you Sandra. I did too, and... good luck.' I kissed her proffered cheek.

Two weeks later my homeward-bound train approached a level crossing, where there was usually a bit of shaking due to the uneven track. This evening the shaking became more pronounced, and then the train decelerated very rapidly, coming to a stop a few hundred yards further on. Some luggage, a couple of laptops, and several coffee cups were thrown about, but none of the passengers appeared injured. The guard and other train staff moved rapidly through the coaches, checking everyone to make sure they were unharmed. Five minutes later the guard came on the intercom, announcing that there had been an 'incident', and the train would remain in place until a relief driver could board. Of course the word went through the carriages that it had probably been a suicide at the level crossing. I always think that's a hellish way to commit suicide;

you're putting the responsibility for your death on the poor bloody train driver. He would have to live with that for the rest of his life, while the suicide is out of it. I called Linda and told her I'd be late home. She said she'd be happy to give Kate and Liam their tea, and to keep them with her until I got there. We were stuck on the train for an hour and a half. I have to confess I was pretty shaken up by the whole business. Linda offered me a hug when I got to her place, and for a moment we just held each other. Her skin smelled warm and spicy and it felt really nice to hold her. *Really* nice.

~ Oc ~

APRIL IS AN ANNUAL JOY in Alan's part of France, the Languedoc, the languid south, the region once separated from the rest of the country by language; their use of 'oc' for yes, while the rest said 'oïl', which became 'oui'. Separated too by their medieval support for the martyred Cathars, the *bonnes hommes*, the *parfaits* and *parfaites*. The season for sowing is over, as is the winter hunting, and the first vine shoots that had broken out in March are now firm young whippy growths ready to be tied in, with fresh green leaves at their tips. There is a warmth in the sunlight, and as the days lengthen there are songs from the young girls walking through the village streets. They seem more beautiful to Alan, in ways which are exciting and dangerous. He decided to take an Easter break in Perpignan, where it is appreciably warmer and the flowers from Spain already fill the florist shops. The women buying them to brighten their homes, know that the heady scents of nectar and pollen will stimulate their husbands, or their lovers, before the heat of summer makes them protest that it is too hot or too tiring to make love. Sex is in the air, almost tangibly, and if he'd had the nose of a dog, it would doubtless have become apparent to him in the morning breeze drifting up from the sea and over the villages along the route.

Strangely, in the light of his past bad-cathedral experiences, Alan always enjoyed the local religious ceremonies. They had an intensity and a totality of participation which impressed him. There was a genuine expression of religious feeling, and although it was something that happened every year there was a spontaneous energy that he had never found in church services back home, at the weddings and funerals he was obliged to attend in Scotland. First, this was an occasion for an intense and solemn procession through the streets. Relics of the saints, in their gold-framed caskets, were brought out and carried, according to their size and weight, on cushions or on more elaborate biers. They were surrounded by the faithful, and preceded by priests swinging heavy censers which emitted their cloying and resinous smoke. The town band, which led each group of petitioners and penitents from church to church, played badly, and out of tune. Alan loved how awful it sounded, and how chaotically the whole event unfolded. From time to time the procession would stop at some specific point, for no apparent reason that he could see, while a prayer was spoken, or a blessing conveyed with brush-swipes of Holy Water. Some of the more fervent in the crowds would shout or sing their own sorrows. People would press forward to touch or kiss a casket, or even just the cushion on which it rested. An attendant stood by with a cloth, wiping between kisses, although his cloth was never cleaned. The combined cacophony reached a crescendo back at the cathedral, before the relics disappeared back into the cool, dark interior. After that the celebrations started in earnest, the band struck up happier tunes, and the teenagers raced around frightening their black-draped grandmothers with firecrackers.

The grannies, having seen it many times before, pretend shock, fear and outrage, as they always do. But they are the same women who, in their youth, had loved as intensely, as explosively, as their younger heirs do these breath-taking spring days, these breathless spring nights. And they remember.

~ Also available in grey ~

WHAT'S WRONG WITH PINK TROUSERS? Why didn't she like me wearing pink trousers? Of course I could be pedantic and say the shade is actually 'crushed raspberry', but I won't deny their fundamental pinkitude.

Pink has no intrinsic meaning; it is simply a colour, a pigment formed by adding white to red. When I was a sannyasin we were always told to wear something red, but nobody ever specified the precise shade. Crimson? Scarlet? Russet? Maroon? I wouldn't ever wear bright red trousers—too Ronald McDonald—but pink is perjink.

There is no logical reason why we say *Pink for Girls, Blue for Boys*. Once all children wore white. Then boys were dressed in pink as often as they were dressed in blue. And some men look good in pink shirts. So why not pink trousers?

'You're illogical. I'm not effeminate, just colourful. Nothing sissy about me, Karen, and you know it. I sing bass in the community choir, don't I? Not just bass, but *second* bass, *really* deep. I'm fully descended, if you know what I mean.'

And Karen laughs that dirty laugh of hers.

I am totally wrapped up in her, exclusively and without a moment's uncertainty. She does it for me, whatever 'it' is, and she always has. She's my wife, my lover, my best friend, my partner, the only woman I'm interested in. And there's a lot to keep my interest alive. She's always different, yet always the same. I try to be interesting for her too.

Then, sitting at the kitchen table, when the children were off to bed, she started *that* conversation.

'John, I need to tell you something.'

'Oh dear, that sounds serious.'

'It *is* serious, so please stop clowning. Remember when we started out, you and I?'

'How could I forget? A lightning strike would have been kinder.'

'Yes, and then we just took off, running away and moving in together. We didn't even tell my parents where we were.'

'Yes, it was a bit embarrassing when the police found us.' She blushed, remembering. 'But Karen, we got over it, and so did your parents, eventually. I think they quite like me now, at least your father does. So where is this leading?'

'Well you knew I was engaged to Bill Inkster at the time?'

'Yes, you told me all about your murky past.'

'Shut up John. What I didn't tell you was that when he found out about us he moved away, took a job in Canada and got married there.'

'Good for him. They're happy?'

'Yes. No family. He never did want children.'

'So?'

'So he's back over for a short trip, seeing his folks. His Dad's got Alzheimer's, so it's probably the last chance to see him before it gets worse.'

'That's a shame.'

'His Mum phoned my Mum, and she gave her my office number.'

'I have a bad feeling about this. I think I can see where this is going.'

'He called me today. He wants to see me tomorrow night. He said we never did get the chance to say goodbye properly, and he wants to do that, to get 'closure', as he put it.'

'Amateur psychologist, is he?'

'He's something in the agriculture business.'

'Arrr, Farmer Bill, come and lubricate my tractor.'

'Stop it John! This is serious.'

'Sorry Karen. I'm getting nervous about what you're saying, if I'm absolutely honest.'

'So am I John, very nervous. But this is something I need to do, for Bill, for me, and for you too. I need to see him again, just the once. I really do think something good will come out of it.'

'I'll reserve judgement. Where are you meeting?'

'His hotel. I'll go there straight from work. Will you give the girls their supper?'

'Of course,' I said. I teach English and Drama at the local comprehensive, and the girls attend the primary school just next door. They're both used to waiting for me in the school if Karen can't pick them up.

'How long will you be?' I asked.

'Ask me something I can answer.'

I have to admit that reply threw me. I mean, how long can it take to say goodbye? Was there something else she needed to do? I tried to work it out but my schedule got in the way. I had papers to mark, and a script to work on for one of my drama lessons. By the time I had finished I was tired and ready for bed.

I wear a sleeping mask at night. I can't sleep when it's light, and the dawn comes far too early in summer. The mask gives me an extra hour or so asleep. Karen won't have blackout curtains. I don't think she'd have curtains at all if it wasn't for the neighbours.

I woke at 6:30, my usual time, and Karen was already

up and about, making packed lunches for the girls, me and herself. She was quite imaginative most of the time, but my lunchbox today just contained bought sandwiches, an apple and a little box of raisins. I normally eat in the staff room, along with most of my colleagues. Karen gave me a coffee-flavoured kiss, picked up her briefcase and laptop, and left to drive to her estate agent job in the market town. Property is something that's mostly a good thing to be in, apart from the negative equity scare of a few years back. It's a steady job, but varied, and she likes it.

Our girls are great; clever, funny and full of personality. I love them to bits, even though they always groan at my jokes. I set out their cereal, fruit juice and yoghurt. Then we went off on the school run, dropping the girls off outside their school before going in to start my day.

It went well for me; Shakespeare and World War I poetry filled the morning, and in the afternoon I had a read-through with our drama group, working on an original script. It's best if they're involved with the writing, as well as the acting. They liked it. And then it was 4:15, time to pick up Sam and Reggie from the after-school club and take them home. I made my world-renowned sausage casserole, but the girls had bigger appetites than I had. I set the leftovers aside to cool down before I put them in the freezer. Then the girls did their homework, watched a bit of telly, and went upstairs for baths and bed. I can rely on them managing for themselves now, and they've both grown out of wanting me to read them stories, although I loved doing that for them when they were little.

I had finished marking my papers by ten, and there was nothing I wanted to watch on TV. I couldn't have a drink, because it was a weekday, and I'd have to be up at 6:30 as usual. But I was unsettled. I half expected Karen to text me that she was on her way home, but there were no messages. I didn't want to text her, in case she'd think I was checking up on her—I didn't want to appear jealous or insecure. They would have gone for a meal somewhere, I guessed, but what else? By eleven I was tired. I locked the door, switched off the downstairs lights and came upstairs, checking my daughters were asleep before going to bed.

I pulled on my sleep mask but sleep didn't come easily, even in the blindfold darkness. I kept wondering where Karen was, and what was happening? Would this thing that she had to do, this 'closure', this goodbye, come between us? Could it harm our family, risk our home and our lives? Would it change Karen? Would it change my love for her? My thoughts went round and round in increasingly toxic circles.

It was the front door closing that woke me. I raised my sleep mask and checked the time. Late, but not *late* late, if you get my drift. I heard her open and close the girls' bedroom doors, checking as I would have done. I pulled my mask down, but left a little gap at the bottom. Karen didn't switch on the bedroom light. She used the *en suite* bathroom and left its light on when she came into the bedroom. She undressed, and stood naked in the middle of the room. She looked across at the bedside chair with my clothes on it, the rumpled shirt I'd wear again next day, my pink trousers folded semi-neatly. I kept my breathing slow, regular, quiet, as in my former meditation routine. She stood looking at me for a long, long time before switching off the bathroom light and slipping into her side of the bed.

~ Carapace ~

IT WAS THE HEAVY BREATHING that aroused her. He was spinning as fast as he could, and his breathing was rapid, shallow and open-mouthed, with rhythmic gasping. It reminded Carol of sex with Mike before they were married, and she could feel her face getting hotter and hotter.

Carol was a regular at the gym, going three times a week, but she hadn't experienced anything like this before. She had started about a year ago, initially to lose some weight, but then to tone up her muscles and to work on her figure. The girls in her office were slim, young, fit, attractive. She was envious but realised that, being older and having had children, she could not compete with them, but she wanted to feel better about herself, and she had quickly got into the exercise habit. Mike thought she might be bored, running on the treadmill, working on the spin bike and using the resistance machines, but she was not. It was a routine, certainly, but she liked the feeling of being pleasantly exhausted at the end of her sessions, and it had made a difference both to her weight and to her figure. And she found, thanks to the endless music videos playing on the gym screens, she was now more familiar with modern pop than she was comfortable with admitting in public. She couldn't be bothered faffing around with her own MP3 player, ditching it after the first month of use. Usually she worked out on her own, but this time there was a young man on the spin bike next to her.

Her neighbour's exercise program seemed to have a lot of hills in it, the rider spinning up to high effort and then down for maximum speed. He would push himself really hard for a minute, bum out of the saddle, and then slow down and relax, his breathing returning to normal. Then he would shift the level up and start pumping again, breathing hard as he did so. Carol guessed it was what they call high intensity training. She felt quite pedestrian, doing her usual fifteen minutes on the spin bike.

She cut her ride short and took a long drink of water before wiping down the saddle and handlebars. Cycling side by side like that, she hadn't really looked at the man before, but now she gave him a surreptitious glance as she took another glug from her water bottle. He was a few years younger than her, quite slim, with taut muscles in his legs. She realised she'd seen him before in the gym, a regular like herself, but she'd never paid any attention to him before. She didn't even know his name.

He was idling back down after his workout, towelling the sweat from his face. His singlet was stained and damp. He smelled, not unpleasantly, of fresh sweat—no cologne that she could detect. 'That looked strenuous,' she said. 'Are you in training for something?'

'Not really,' he replied. 'I just like to keep fit. I sit behind a desk all day, so this is my only exercise. I'm Terry by the way,' and he offered his hand.

She shook it. 'Carol,' she told him. 'You live around here?'

'We moved in to one of the new houses around six months ago.'

'Nice.'

'Yes, the town's got a lot of facilities, I can commute to work by train, and the primary school is handy for the kids. Are you local?'

'Yes, we've been here nearly ten years, in one of the older

properties.' She thought it best to finish the conversation before it became awkward or led in a direction she didn't want it to go. 'Well, I'm going on the cross-trainer for ten minutes, and then I'll have a swim. I'll see you around, Terry.'

Two evenings later he was there again. She sat on her spin bike and he came over, said hello, and sat on the bike next to her. He started off with a quick sprint, then he pushed up the little 'effort' lever and went for the high resistance setting. Pretty soon he was out of the saddle and puffing hard. Carol didn't feel so embarrassed or, frankly, turned on, this time. She raised herself out of the saddle, pushed her hands out to grasp the handlebar extensions at the front, and switched to high speed cycling. Soon she was breathing as hard as Terry, but she had a sly smile on her face. She wondered if her own heavy breathing would have a similar effect on him.

They both stopped at more or less the same time, wiped down the bikes and towelled their gleaming faces. 'That was fun, Terry. Were you trying to make a race of it?'

'Guilty as charged,' he said with a laugh. 'Who do you think won?'

'Oh, I'm sure you did, but if we do the cross-trainers next I might get to even up the score,' she said.

They worked out together for the rest of their hour then, before heading off to the showers, he asked her if she fancied a coffee in the café afterwards. She agreed. She really did enjoy the novelty of talking to someone else in the gym, and he hadn't said anything to suggest he was interested in her for anything other than conversation. They were both grown-ups. There was nothing wrong with two adults having a conversation over coffee, honestly. It didn't mean anything more than that.

'I've never had a workout partner before, but that was really good tonight. If you ever feel like doing it again, I'd appreciate it.'

'Why don't we try if for a couple of weeks, and see how it works out? It was good to be challenged, Terry.'

'And you challenged me too, Carol. That was fun. Let's compare diaries and see if we can work out a schedule.'

They discovered they both liked gym sessions three evenings every week, and agreed Monday, Wednesday and Thursday would work well for both of them, allowing for the inevitable days when they could not meet. It wouldn't be a problem for either of them if the other didn't show up for some reason. She brought her exercise notebook, and they compared notes to see what each of them wanted to work on. They both liked to start with an aerobic session, so they settled on spin bikes and cross-trainers first, then Carol wanted to row, and Terry wanted to work on his glutes, so he would do the stepper. Carol thought she could try the step machine too, to tone up her thighs and bottom. Then they could work on the resistance machines and free weights. They decided that they'd each see what they wanted to do, and work out a programme between them. They would 'spot' each other on the free weights. It's always best to work with a partner when you're lifting heavy weights, someone to grab the bar if you've over-reached yourself on the bench press.

'Where do you work, Terry?' she asked.

'Century Finance.'

'Never. I don't believe it. That's where I work too,' she told him.

'What do you do there?'

'I'm in HR.'

'I'm in the financial analysis team. It's a good company. I've been there nearly four years now.'

'I've never seen you in the office,' she said.

'Well, apart from emails, the only contact I've had with HR was in my first week. A girl dressed all in black. I thought she looked like Morticia, from the Addams Family.'

'There are three of them, and they all dress alike. Some folk call them the Weird Sisters, only they're not related, and they're really not particularly weird.'

'But you don't dress that way?'

'No, as Head of HR I feel I have to wear a suit.'

'Goodness! You're one of the bosses?'

'It seems so Terry.'

'I'll make sure I keep in your good books then.'

They laughed and said their farewells. Of course, when Carol got in to the office next day she checked out his profile. A hard worker, not a high flyer, but as solid as a rock, with good performance reviews for the past three years. Married, with a young family. Dependable. She sat back in her chair and asked herself why she was checking up on him. She felt guilty. Was she thinking about some kind of affair with him? A fling? She couldn't imagine it. Before she came to a conclusion her three senior female colleagues returned from their tea break. She remembered Terry mentioning Morticia, and wondered which of her witches he had meant. Dress-wise, they were pretty much interchangeable, all in black skirts and black tops. OK, it wasn't particularly unusual wear for an office, but they did look a bit like Goths, except without the tattoos and Goth make-up.

None of them liked Carol, although they'd never say it out loud. The prettiest witch, Lisa, was her deputy, and she definitely hated Carol. She had tried to upstage her when she first started in the department, but Carol was the one who wrote her annual review, and she made that clear to her. She could seethe in private but it wouldn't make any difference. Carol also happened to know Lisa was in an ongoing relationship with one of the senior people in the investment section, a married man. Lisa wasn't certain that Carol knew about it, but a couple of rather unsubtle hints had been dropped at one point, when she was crowding Carol over something, and she backed off immediately. It could cause her a lot of problems if that ever became public. Lisa fancied having Carol's job one day, but Carol had a long time to go before retirement. Lisa was actually very capable—the whole coven of them were, or they wouldn't have lasted as long as they had in HR. Carol had a reputation for toughness, and she cultivated it assiduously. It helped that she was part of the senior team in Corporate Services, along with the Finance and Property heads. They met weekly with John Templeton, their Director, so she was in the loop for all policy and strategy issues. She loved working at this level; it energised her and made her feel confident.

She had grown her career through finding and exercising her abilities, taking on new duties and responsibilities, and carrying them out well. She had come to believe that there were very few challenges in life that she couldn't rise to, given enough time and training.

She had never been one to socialise with her work colleagues out of hours. Family, a husband, and the fact that she lived quite a bit outside the city made it difficult. Besides, Carol believed it was not a good idea for any of the HR team to get too close to colleagues in other departments. But one Wednesday afternoon, after she and Patricia had finished interviewing candidates for a vacancy in Finance, Patricia raised the subject.

'I know you don't often come out for office do's, but Lisa and I have started going round the corner to the Green Tree once a week after work for a couple of drinks. They have a Happy Hour on a Friday, and it's a chance to unwind. I wondered if you'd like to join us some time?'

Carol was a bit flummoxed, but being put on the spot like that she couldn't think of an acceptable reason to say no, so she said she couldn't manage that Friday, but could go the following week, as long as it finished early enough to get the train home.

'We're normally there from 5 until 6 for the cheap drinks, then we grab a bite to eat and head home. Some of the young ones make a night of it, dancing and stuff, but we don't—you know I'm married, and Lisa always has things to do. You'll like it Carol.'

'Who else goes?' I asked.

'About a dozen or so usually. Mostly from Finance, a few others from the investments side.'

Carol thought about it, and decided she was right. Mike would watch the kids quite happily, and she liked the thought of having some 'me' time. Patricia wasn't particularly challenging, and she knew she could handle Lisa.

'OK Patricia, a week on Friday I'll join you.'

In the meantime she continued with her gym routine. The harder sessions she was doing with Terry had made her lose more weight and gain muscle tone, and she liked the changes in her body. Even Mike noticed.

'You know Carol, you're looking very sexy these days. Maybe I should join you at the gym?'

'Maybe you should, but we'd have to take the children with us, unless you're planning on making them work out too?'

'Well, maybe I could go at the weekends? You've always got shopping and housework going on, so it would be fine. What do you think?'

'You're looking pretty good yourself these days Mike. Have you been training at lunch-times?'

'No, but I have cut out the beer.'

'Good for you. Speaking of drinks, are you OK to put Allie and Eric to bed a week on Friday? My coven has invited me out for a couple of drinks.'

'Sure, that's fine. It's never a problem looking after the kids.'

'Thanks Mike, I'll make it up to you.'

'Ooh, promises, promises.' He laughed.

On the following Friday Carol, Patricia and Lisa finished work slightly early and walked round to the Green Tree pub. Carol hadn't wanted to dress up too differently from her normal office wear, a dark trouser suit, but she'd put on a blue silk scarf for a splash of colour, knowing it would be a contrast to the funereal garb of her colleagues.

They settled in to their seats at a table. Lisa and Patricia were on pints, and Carol had a glass of white wine. The bar was already crowded, and she recognised several colleagues from the other departments in the company. Ronnie, the man Lisa was seeing, came over to join them, but maintained a distance between himself and Lisa. Carol knew him, of course. She tended to know most of the senior people.

'Nice of you to join us Carol. You've not been here before?'

'No, I live quite far out in the sticks, so it's not convenient. My last train's at 9 o'clock during the week, so I don't have the time. And there's the children too.'

'Who's babysitting this time?'

'My husband Mike.'

'Two of mine are at university, and the other two are sixteen and seventeen, so they don't need babysitting. Yours must be much younger.'

'Allison—Allie—is twelve and Eric's ten.'

Ronnie was very pleasant, a good-looking man with hair beginning to show silver-grey at the sides. His face was tanned and smooth, and his grey eyes sparkled. Damn, Carol thought, why do some men age better than women? He was very easy to talk to, and she could see how Lisa had been attracted to him, but he seemed very much a family man.

Carol needed to go to the ladies, and Lisa came with her. She found herself saying that Ronnie seemed very nice.

'Oh, he is. I like him a lot, but there's no way he'd leave his wife for me. I'm actually happy with being his occasional bit on the side. It suits me—I don't ever want to settle down with anyone. You'll keep this between ourselves Carol, won't you?'

'Of course, it goes no further.'

'Good. And I won't say anything about Terry.'

Carol was shocked and confused. 'But it's not... there's nothing ... I mean, we just work out at the gym.'

'Relax Carol, I'm just pulling your chain. I know you're not having an affair with him, you're just gym buddies. But you have to admit it could look like something else to people who don't know you.'

'How did you find out?'

'Ronnie told me. Terry's one of his protégés. They get together every month.'

'Has Terry said anything to him about me?'

'Just that you push each other at the gym. He thinks you're good for each other, and he likes you. He's very wrapped up in his wife and the little ones though.'

'Yes I know, just as I'm wrapped up with my family.' They looked at each other. Carol's mind was racing.

'We'd better get back before they send out a search party,' said Lisa.

When they got back to the table Ronnie had set up another round of drinks; white wine for Carol and beer for the younger women. Lisa sat closer to him now, and Carol realised that many of their colleagues knew about the affair, had known for some time, but couldn't care less about it. These things happen, no need to make a fuss. It was fairly common these days, taken for granted by most people. The lovers hadn't drawn attention to it, but they hadn't hidden it either. It began to dawn on Carol that she really would have to tell Mike about Terry, and convince him it wasn't an affair. It was a friendship, and would never be anything more than that, but it was a secret friendship, and with secrecy came guilt. She didn't want to feel guilty, there was no reason for it. She just had to tell Mike what she was doing on three evenings every week. How difficult could that be?

She caught the eight o'clock train and was home half an hour later. She hadn't felt like eating earlier, but she was hungry now. She grabbed a slice of bread and plastered it with home-made damson jam before wolfing it down. Then she had another. Lips and tongue stained red, and face flushed with the wine, she walked through to the lounge, where Mike was watching something boring on the telly. He switched it off and turned to her.

'How was it?'

'Good. Informative. Maybe even enlightening, I'd say.'

'Sounds interesting. You've got some insights into your colleagues then?'

'And maybe into myself.'

'How so?' he asked.

'Well, I think I've maybe created a shell around myself without realising it, made myself appear unapproachable or aloof, too tough maybe.'

'Wow, that's quite something for a couple of G and T's to achieve.'

'White wine actually, but the effect was the same. I've decided to try to be a bit more open, at work, and maybe at home too.'

'Really?'

'Yes, here too. And I'm going to start with something that feels quite awkward, but shouldn't be.'

'Go on,' he said.

'About the gym.' She paused. He looked at her quizzically. 'I have a confession,' she said.

'Really?'

'Yes. The reason I've toned up recently is that I've been working out with a training partner, a work colleague.'

'One of your coven?'

'No. It's a man called Terry Evans from our investment bank side. He moved here six months ago with his family.

I'd seen him around, but I never knew we worked for the same company.'

'What do you do ... as training partners, I mean?'

'We work out together on the spin bikes, the cross-trainers and the free weights. We've been sort of competing, pushing each other, and it's definitely been good for me.'

Mike seemed to be working things out in his head. 'Do you see him... outside of the gym?'

'No. There is absolutely nothing going on between us, and there never will be. It's just we both enjoy working out together. I think you like the results. But I think you should meet him. I like him, and I think you'll like him too. I've been wrong not to tell you about this, but I don't want us to have any secrets. We could maybe have their family round some weekend, go to McDonald's or something. Their kids are younger than ours.'

'Yes, Wilma told me about them.'

'Wilma?'

'Terry's wife, of course. We go out running together when we can get away from the kids. She's very nice. You'll like her. And she asked me to thank you.'

'To thank me? What for?'

'She's says you've revved up their sex life since you started working out with him. He comes home excited and can't get enough of her. And I love running with her, seeing her in that racerback bra and Lycra running shorts. It works for me too, you know.'

'How did you start ... meeting her?'

'She phoned me. Terry told her about meeting you that first time, but she wasn't sure what your intentions were. I have to admit when you said nothing about him I wasn't sure either. We just decided to go with the flow until you came clean. I was confident you would eventually, unless you had an ulterior motive. I'm very glad you haven't.'

'No, I haven't. Thank you, I think,' Carol said.

~ Ash ~

BERNARD (SOMETIMES BERNIE) and Geraldine (never abbreviated) were sitting on separate armchairs in their living room, discussing their wedding. They were the kind of couple friends would say were "made for each other", but both were just a little too large to share a two-seater couch without a crush. For him it had been love at first sight. For her it was also love, but she had done the calculations first. She had sold her flat and moved in with him three years before, using the money from her property sale to put into a savings account, in her name naturally, because that was just so much more convenient, she had explained. Bernard was a big man, an ex-rugby player, but his days spent behind a desk in the Council's Planning Department had left him considerably less fit than he used to be. Geraldine, an office worker in the same Council's Social Work Department, was what well-meaning friends described as "comfortable". Bernard's recent promotion accelerated their decision to marry. Was it her suggestion, or had he suddenly made up his mind about the future of their relationship? He couldn't remember, but it didn't really matter at the end of the day. It was all very lovey-dovey for the nearly-weds that evening, and for months afterwards, until the night Geraldine mentioned the phone call from her sister Flo.

Three weeks until the wedding, just three short weeks! She should have said no. When Flo asked Geraldine to pop over to Germany to babysit her nieces for a week, she could just have said no, it was too close to the wedding. But she didn't.

She's a phenomenally good organiser, Geraldine, it's why she's so highly thought of at work.

'I can easily do this, Bernie, it's just a week—not even a full week, just six days. We'll have two clear days before the wedding, plenty of time to tick off the last few things. I'm well ahead. Look.'

She had a checklist for the wedding tasks, with dates by which they needed to be completed, and sure enough most of them had ticks in the 'Completed' boxes. She could have completed them all in plenty of time, allowing for unforeseen circumstances.

Bernard needed to work right up until two days before the wedding, so his tasks were fewer and much easier to plan and organise. His annual leave would account for a full three weeks, and their honeymoon was planned for two of those weeks. Somewhere warm, they thought, somewhere exotic, tropical. Dominican Republic? Ideal.

Geraldine would be home on the Thursday at lunchtime, and her hen night was planned for that evening, giving her Friday to recover before their wedding on the Saturday. She hadn't told him what was planned for that evening, but she would stay overnight with her friend Julia. His stag night was in her checklist for the same evening, but he hadn't told her his plans either. She assumed he'd be out with his mates, getting plastered, then allowing them to tie him naked to a lamp-post in the middle of town—the usual thing. In fact, he been to enough stag nights in his time to know he wasn't interested in having one. He didn't drink much, he didn't like being around drunks, and he hated the sort of testosterone-fuelled behaviour that goes on at these things. In the weeks before the wedding his best man John had repeatedly asked him where he wanted to go for his stag night, but Bernard told him he just wasn't interested in having one. He asked John not to let Geraldine know, and since they didn't really get on, Bernard was sure he hadn't. Everything seemed to be taken care of, and Geraldine flew out to Frankfurt. She phoned him that evening, just to say she had arrived, and she'd begin her baby-sitting duties the next day. Flo had to travel to a conference in Rome, and her husband was off on one of his globe-trotting business jaunts in Asia. Geraldine would look after Flo's young daughters, and Flo would be back on the Wednesday evening, in time to drive Geraldine to the airport early on the Thursday morning. It seemed to Bernard to be cutting things very fine, but he was a natural worrier. What if there was a baggage handlers' dispute? What about stroppy French air traffic controllers? Geraldine's calmness and efficiency just washed over his concerns.

'It'll be fine. It's all organised. Stop worrying.'

He stopped worrying. And then a little-known Icelandic volcano called Eyjafjällajökull blew its top, spewing thousands of tons of fine volcanic ash high into the atmosphere. By the next day UK airspace was closed, and no planes could get in or out. Geraldine phoned him.

'It'll be all right by tomorrow, Bernie.'

But of course it wasn't. The numbers of flight cancellations swiftly backed up, and it was clear that it would take days to sort out, long after the eruption had finished, which it showed no sign of doing. Geraldine's phone calls became increasingly frantic and then, on the Tuesday evening, the Met Office said that there were signs that the wind direction was changing, and they hoped British airspace could re-open on Wednesday night. He relayed that news to Geraldine, and she contacted Lufthansa for confirmation that

47

she could still get out on Thursday morning as planned. They were non-committal, and suggested she keep checking the internet and phone early the next day.

The winds did change on the Wednesday, but in an easterly direction, blowing the ash plume over the continent. Now German airspace was closed, and they said it would be at least 24 hours before the situation could be reviewed.

Most people have heard about the eruption, and to them it's just a little footnote in history, if anything, but to those who were affected by it, it was a massive disruption in their lives.

Thursday morning came, and the wind had swung back to the west. Now German airspace was open again, but British airspace was closed. Geraldine wasn't going anywhere. Bernard phoned her friend Julia, and told her Geraldine wouldn't make the hen night, and he had concerns about the wedding going ahead.

'Oh no,' she wailed. 'We've booked a club, with a meal, and a band. What'll we do?'

'Just go ahead and have a party by yourselves,' he suggested.

'We've booked a male stripper for her too,' she said, and then immediately realised she'd spilled the beans and hung up hurriedly. A stripper? For Geraldine? Bernard played through a number of scenarios in his head. What would Geraldine get up to with a stripper? What kind of party would it have been? He decided he'd have to have a serious discussion with the bride-to-be, when he eventually saw her. But with all the news reports coming in about stranded travellers, and huge backlogs of flight cancellations everywhere in Europe, it was clear Geraldine wouldn't get back in time for the wedding. He'd have to cancel it. And the honeymoon. He gritted his teeth and made the phone calls. They lost the lot. Her parents were upset but understanding, and they weren't paying for it anyway. Fortunately, it was always intended to be a low-key affair, with about thirty friends and relatives coming to the reception. He lost most of what he'd paid out due to late cancellation. The companies said they were sorry, but there was nothing they could do about it.

Geraldine got home on the following Tuesday. He picked her up at the airport. She had been crying.

'I'm so sorry Bernard.' His Sunday name—she must be upset. 'I was so sure it would be all right.'

'It wasn't though Geraldine. You're not infallible, are you?'

'No.'

'Well, let's get home and get you unpacked. We can go out for a meal tonight and talk about the future. Does that sound all right?' She nodded.

She didn't have much to unpack. Her carry-on case had contained the bare minimum for a six-day stay in Germany, and she had washed her clothes at her sister's place after finding herself trapped for the extra days. Travelling ultra-light was part of her organising habit. No hold luggage means no hanging about in Baggage Reclaim. No heavy laptop, just her tablet and a phone for communications.

They didn't start talking until they were seated in their favourite Cantonese restaurant and they'd ordered their food. Sipping his green tea Bernard started: 'Well then, Geraldine, we know what happened, and we can't do anything to change that, so there's no need to discuss it, but what happens next?'

'We reschedule the wedding?' she said.

'That would be the logical thing to do, the sensible thing, if it's what we both want. But let's see if we really do want that.' He knew he'd shocked her. On top of the upset caused by the volcano, he was questioning their whole relationship. She hadn't seen that one coming either.

'We've been living together for three years now,' he continued. 'I'm happy with that arrangement, but you said you wanted marriage. Was it to keep your parents happy, or was there something else?'

'I want children, Bernie. I want our children. I've seen it from experience in social work that children benefit in many ways from being born into a stable marriage, rather than a live-in arrangement. I've thought about the best time for me to take a career break, and that would probably be in about eighteen months. And after a two-year gap I would want another. I think we should stop at two. I calculate by the time they're ready to go to university we'll both be at our highest earning potential, so we'll be able to support them fully.'

'You've got it all worked out, haven't you?' She blushed.

'I know you think I'm too methodical, but it's just the way I am. I like to know what I'm doing, where I'm going.'

'It doesn't leave you any room for just being spontaneous, does it?'

'And you want that?'

'Sometimes I do Geraldine. And you can't predict exactly when children will come along, if they do.'

'Are you saying you don't want to marry me now?' Their first courses arrived. They were both very hungry, so they wolfed everything down quickly before getting back to their discussion.

'I love you Geraldine, and I want a lifelong relationship

with you. I want children too. I do want to marry you, but you need to recognise that we don't always have the same outlook on life all the time. I don't want my life planned for me. I'm not prepared to tick-box my life. Sometimes I want things to be different, to change, to surprise me.'

'I love you too Bernie, and I want to be your wife and the mother of our children. Sitting in that flat in Frankfurt, trapped by the volcano, with my nieces asleep in their beds, Flo in Rome and you here, I panicked for the first time in my life. I realised there was nothing I could do to influence the situation, it was completely out of my hands. That frightened me, and I hated it. There was no fall-back, no Plan B. I almost went to pieces, but I couldn't let myself go because the kids were sleeping next door. I'm sorry Bernie. I know deep down I shouldn't be like this.'

'Like what Geraldine?'

'Like I have to control everything. I shouldn't. But I can't help it.'

'So...' he began, and at that point their main courses arrived. They both loved Cantonese food, and tended to over-indulge. 'This is good,' he said. 'I've been living on ready meals for a week. Let's finish talking when we get home.' She agreed, and they ate until they couldn't manage another grain of rice between them. It's what they always did in this restaurant.

Bernard felt totally stuffed when they got home. They sat together on the couch, holding hands. He began. 'Have you still got the wedding checklist? Let me see it please.' She fetched it from her home filing cabinet, and he started to skim through it. Then he tore it in half, then into quarters, then strips, which he threw in the bin.

'Ask me what I want,' he said.

'All right,' she said nervously. 'What do you want?'

'I want to marry you.' She gave a sigh of relief. He saw a tear starting in the corner of her eye. He hurried on. 'I want us to go to the local Registrar, explain what's happened, and make the arrangements to reschedule. We shouldn't have to wait, because all the legal requirements have been met. We could be married privately, without fuss, this week. Would that work for you?'

'Yes, I think it would.' She was smiling, then she laughed at the novelty of it. 'We could get our parents to be witnesses. They're the only ones who have to know.' She was getting excited by the idea.

'No best man, and no bridesmaid. No Julia.'

'OK,' she said.

'No hen night, and definitely no stripper.' She blushed. 'Some day you'll have to tell me what that was all about. No honeymoon. We stay together for the rest of our holidays, and then we stay together for the rest of our lives.'

'That's what I want too.'

'Next year we'll go somewhere tropical for a holiday.' She smiled again. 'Unless you're pregnant.' Her face took on a worried look, then she relaxed. In that area of their lives, she was definitely the one in control. They snuggled together for a while, as he stroked her soft brown hair.

'You think I can change, Bernie? Just like that? Become a completely different person?'

'No, I don't, but I think we can work together more, make our decisions joint ones. You have a business plan for our marriage, don't you?'

'I wouldn't call it that, but I do like to plan things in advance.'

'Don't. Not for our lives Geraldine, not for our marriage.

Please. Let's just start with each other, and take things as they come. Do you think we can do that?'

'I'll try. But you need to tell me what you want more often.'

'I'll do that. You know what I like about volcanoes Geraldine?'

'What?'

'They're not about blowing things up, they're about making new land. I want to visit Iceland and get a piece of Eyjafjällajökull ash, and make it into an ornament for our bedroom.'

'That'll be nice, but you'll have to learn to pronounce it properly.'

'I can. It's pronounced *Where-the-hell-did-that-come-from?*'

~ Beached ~

SOFT, WET SAND SQUISHED UP BETWEEN Vickie's toes. She smiled. It was good to give in to pure sensation, to let go of her thoughts, to just live in the moment. It brought back memories of growing up in the little seaside town, and most of the memories were happy ones. Her rebellious teenage memories weren't quite so happy, but she put them aside.

To the residents of course, it wasn't a holiday town. The cafés, ice-cream parlours, chip shops, pubs and gift shops were there all year round, but the locals tended to avoid them in the peak season. They were too noisy and crowded in summer to be pleasant. But the harbour and beach were always beautiful at any time of the year. In the off season, when some businesses closed up and others reduced their hours, the town belonged to the locals.

Their parents had moved there when Vickie and her sister Lynn were toddlers. Vickie was the oldest at three, and Lynn just a year younger. Father was a GP in the nearby market town, and Mum taught in the primary school. Mum was just Mum, but their dad was always Father. At times he could be a rather austere presence, but they knew he loved them.

Vickie had always enjoyed walking along the beach at low tide, feeling that first shock of cold sea water oozing up and over her bare feet, then getting used to the temperature. She liked the 'give' in the sand, quite firm at first, then turning fluid as she wiggled her feet, her weight displacing the water from between the sand grains. When she was young she never built sand castles or sand sculptures. She knew such constructions would always be washed away by the next tide, so she dismissed the activity as pointless and illogical. But walking was different. She could smell the sea, hear the gulls, feel the onshore breeze on her face. The beach was about a mile long, quite enough for a good walk, and quiet enough to have long silent conversations with herself.

Her own children had always loved visiting Granny and Grandpa in their seaside home, then just Granny after Father died. And now Granny was dead too, and she was here to clear the house and sort out the estate with Mum's old lawyer friend. Lynn was working in Italy, and couldn't get away. Of course she couldn't—silly of Vickie to even think about it. Her eldest daughter Jenny was off at university, and her ex-husband had agreed to look after the two younger children, who were still attending school. It was uncharacteristically kind of Roger to offer to look after them, but she knew her younger two didn't like the new woman in Roger's life. They would come back happy to see her, she hoped.

It was Roger's affair that had put the final nail in the coffin of their marriage, but the truth was it had already died years earlier.

The first two days of Vickie's visit were exhausting. She lost count of the number of trips to the recycling depot and the town's charity shops. She worked methodically; storage cupboards first, then room by room clearance. Lynn wasn't sentimental either, so Vickie had no qualms about dumping stuff, even if it had personal connections with either of them. To be honest there was nothing of real value left in the house, not the furniture, not the carpets, not the ornaments—especially not the ornaments. She had the key for mother's 'hidey-hole' in the wall of the *en suite* bathroom, and she'd gone through it. Costume jewellery in the main, but there were a couple of nice rings and some ear-rings she could see herself wearing. She put them in her suitcase to take home. Unwanted furniture was left in the cleared rooms, and the lawyer said he'd organise a local factotum to pick them up for recycling or disposal in a few weeks, before the house was put up for sale. Clothing was easy— straight to the charity shops. The linen cupboard was emptied quickly too. By the third day she felt able to take a break and walk through the town, before going down on the beach to let the childhood memories flood back with the tide.

She walked up to the High Street and put her sandals on. A cup of coffee would be nice, she thought, so she popped in to the café. The man behind the counter looked at her rather more intensely than she was comfortable with, but when he brought the coffee over he seemed to make up his mind to say something.

'Excuse me if I'm being rude, but you remind me of someone who used to live here.' He wiped his hands on his apron. 'You're not Vickie Ellis, by any chance?'

'Yes, I am …well, I was… well I still am actually,' she stammered.

'I don't believe it. I'm Joe Armstrong, we were in the same class in primary school. Remember me?'

'Joe? Really? Oh, that's fantastic. Do you have time for a chat?'

'Of course Vickie, just let me wipe these empty tables and I'll come over.'

She'd noticed when she came in that the café was due to close at 4, and it was now 3.30. Joe turned the sign to

CLOSED, locked the door, and came over to the table with his own cup of coffee and a slice of cake for each of them.

'What brings you back to town, Vickie?'

'Clearing Mum's house. I should be finished tomorrow, then I'll see the lawyer and head home.'

'Yes of course. I was sorry to hear about your mum, I always got on with her. Are you... on your own?' he asked.

Vickie smiled at his obvious diffidence. 'Here, yes. At home, no. I've got a girl and a boy at school, and another girl at university.'

'Hubby looking after the family?'

'Yes, thankfully. We're divorced, but he's still their Dad. Are you married Joe?'

'Was, but she died three years ago. Breast cancer. My son is in the army. He joined up the year after Lucy died. He's abroad just now, but he won't tell me where. Special forces.'

'Lucy?'

'Lucy Punton. I don't know if you remember her from school?'

'Of course I do. She was one of the gang, a real live wire, great fun, up for anything, wasn't she? Oh, I'm so sorry Joe, I shouldn't be talking about her like that. Forgive me.'

'It's all right Vickie. I had a long time to get used to the thought of losing her before she died. We talked about it a lot. She made me promise to get over her and move on with my life.'

'And did you?'

'Not entirely, but I'm trying. I gave up my job, moved back here and bought the café. It's hectic in the summer, but in the winter it's usually just the locals, and that's more relaxed. I enjoy cooking, so that side of it keeps me interested. I do a different lunch special every day, as well as soups and salads. I've got my regulars. You'll know some of them. Come back in for lunch tomorrow and you'll meet them.'

'I'll do that Joe. Well, that was really nice meeting you again, and thanks for the cake. Did you bake it yourself?'

'Yes, a Victoria sponge—isn't that appropriate Vickie?' He laughed, and she smiled at him, comfortable in his company, before heading back to Mum's house for a quiet meal on her own. On impulse she bought a bottle of white wine from the Co-op. After meeting Joe she felt like having a reminiscence night, and the wine would help with that.

Vickie and her friends, including Lucy Punton, were a proper little gang of tearaways at primary school. Vickie was one of the leaders, having a very forceful personality even at that age. She would never back down on anything, to anybody. They'd done lots of things together—swimming, beach games, lighting bonfires in the sand dunes, jumping in the sea from the harbour walls, sneaking up on courting couples and once or twice catching them in the act. But after primary school Vickie was sent away to boarding school, which she hated, and she lost touch with her local friends. Her parents never encouraged her to keep in contact with them, so she never did. Besides, she had a whole new group of classmates—all girls—who shared what she felt to be the misery of boarding school. And there she was no longer the leader of anything; that was made clear to her right at the start.

For the first few years she behaved herself, but by fifteen her hormones were kicking in, and she became rebellious and difficult. Sneaking away from school was never easy, although she and some friends managed it a few times. But like *The Great Escape*, they were soon recaptured and rounded up, with letters going to the parents. Father came to the school for a meeting with the Head Teacher. Mum, who was a Head Teacher herself by then, was too embarrassed to come, according to Father. Vickie had to promise to buckle down and study for her exams, to show respect for her teachers, and to behave herself. She fumed, but she did behave, mostly. She studied hard, and successfully disguised her contempt for the teaching staff. One out of three wasn't bad.

She had avoided being expelled by the skin of her teeth, but she did well enough in her exams to be admitted to university to study medicine, much to Father's pleasure. At least at uni she was independent, as those were the happy days of student grants. But the independence led to drink, and drink led to dancing, and dancing led to sex, and sex led to pregnancy and a hasty marriage to Roger, the cad, the man her parents were convinced had ruined her. They weren't entirely wrong.

Roger was in his final year studying architecture when they met. He was older, more experienced than her previous few lovers, and he thought the sun shone out of his backside. Vickie was smitten by him. Maybe her boarding school experience had reduced her confidence? Or maybe he just caught her when her defences were low? She didn't know, but he did agree to marry Vickie when she told him she was pregnant.

She loved being a mum, and lavished loads of time, energy and affection on Jenny, then Anne, and finally Lachlan. Meanwhile Roger had started on his meteoric rise as an architect, joining a good firm, attracting interest with his designs, becoming the youngest ever partner in the practice, and earning a lot of money, too much of which he spent on himself. Along the way he became cool towards Vickie, and she discovered he'd been having an affair with one of his colleagues. On reflection, Vickie thought it probably wasn't his first, but it was the first one she'd found out about. When she confronted him he admitted it, but said it would fizzle out and they'd be back to normal 'in the fullness of time'. That was a situation she couldn't live with. They divorced and he remarried. Vickie rented a small flat and looked after the children, working as a receptionist in the health centre. She couldn't keep away from medicine altogether.

Enough sad memories! She poured another glass of wine, and walked round the house, her footsteps echoing in the empty rooms. They were large rooms, much bigger than in the modern flat she occupied in the city. They still had the smell she associated with the word 'home', and she felt a tear come into her eye. Stop it Vickie, she said to herself, you're a no-nonsense adult with a good brain, hardened by the things life has hit you with. Don't get sentimental now. But she wasn't sentimental, not really. This *was* a lovely house, built in the seaside boom of the Edwardian period. It was solid. It had value. It had the potential to become a comfortable family home. With Mum's ornaments and knick-knacks out of it, and only the hideous wallpaper to remind Vickie of 1960s fashions, she could see herself living here again, maybe with a new kitchen and bathroom, and there'd be room for the kids too. She went to bed slightly drunk, but a lot less anxious than she had been at the beginning of the week.

She made an appointment to see the lawyer next day. She had a fair idea how much her share of the estate would be, and it was to be split equally between Vickie and

Lynn—there were no other beneficiaries. She explained to him that she was thinking of buying out Lynn's share of the house and going to live there for a time, and he agreed to handle the legal side of things if Lynn would go along with it. Vickie was fairly sure she would; she'd always had an unhealthy liking for money, and it would uncomplicate her life if she had more to spend on fashionable handbags and accessories.

And then it was lunch-time, and she braced herself for a visit to Joe's café, and potential encounters with schoolmates. It was crowded, but Joe sat her beside Avril and Denise, two old chums, and they laughed their way through bowls of Joe's tasty vegetable soup, with good chunky bread. Avril talked about her job as practice manager at the local health centre.

'It's getting busier, with all the new houses being built on the south side of the town. I think we'll need a new receptionist soon, and maybe another GP.'

'I'm a receptionist, Avril, and you know I did three years of a medical degree before I got married. If I came back to live here, do you think you might consider me for a part-time job?'

'I'll talk to the team, but I think you'd be ideal.' They exchanged details, and Vickie told her which practice she was working in, so she could get a reference.

She had to go home to collect Anne and Lachlan from their father's home on the Friday, and they picked up clothes, bedding and supplies from the flat before driving down to Mum's house, although Vickie was already calling it 'my house' in her mind. She'd put the disposal of furniture on hold, so the house was still furnished, albeit in an old-fashioned style, but that was OK. Vickie put her things in

Mum's bedroom, Anne's in the guest room, and Lachlan's in Father's old study bedroom. The kids loved it, and on the Saturday morning they walked along the beach together. Vickie and Anne slipped off their shoes and walked barefoot. Lachlan kept his trainers on, but that was typical. He had more of Roger's personality in him than Anne, but he was a much nicer person than his father.

She told them her idea about moving there, and they were enthusiastic. They enjoyed Joe's lasagne too, and Avril slipped in to the café to ask Vickie when she could manage an interview with the senior GP. After that, things seemed to move very quickly.

By the time she had lived there for a month or so, Joe and Vickie had become very close. He moved in with her, and that was a bit of a revelation for her too. A man who wasn't dashing about all over the place doing important architecty things, but who had a job he was happy in, worked in her own town, and who now had a warm place in her life.

These days people might come across them walking barefoot on the shore or lighting barbecue fires in the sand dunes. They don't sneak around looking for couples having sex in the dunes though. There's no need for that, not with their own fine bedroom with a wonderful sea view.

~ The Sting ~

IT WAS STILL TOO SHALLOW to swim. Normally David would have waited until the shock of cold water suddenly coming in contact with his genitals told him it was time to strike out, in that laboured breast stroke of his. Here, in the little bay in Brittany, the beach shelved away so gradually that he and Hugh had to wade out a couple of hundred metres. He watched a baby flounder, disturbed by his footfall, skitter away over the sand, in the sun-warmed water. He did not see the sharp point sticking out of the sand, but he felt an excruciating pain in the pad of his big toe, so bad he almost passed out. He called out, and Hugh turned towards him.

'What's the matter?'

'Don't know. Stepped on something sharp. Think I'll head back.'

'OK. I'll carry on and swim. Will you be all right?'

'Yes, I'll check it out back at the cottage.' He looked down at his foot. 'It doesn't seem to be bleeding anyway. No blood in the water.'

He hobbled back to the beach, walking on the side of his foot. Sitting on his towel, he cradled his foot and looked at his toe, but could see nothing obvious. Back at the holiday cottage he showered and put on his reading glasses to examine his toe, but his foot was too far away from his eyes. He thought he saw a small black spot, but he couldn't be certain. He would ask his wife to have a proper look at it when she got back from her shopping trip to Audierne. The gîte, their holiday home for the week, went under some unpronounceable Breton name. It was a modern bungalow, in a small development of half a dozen holiday homes, a few kilometres from the pretty little fishing village. David sat on the terrace in his shorts, taking the sun, with his foot resting on a low table. The pain had lessened in intensity, but his toe still throbbed.

Hugh came back from his swim, took off his knee-length red swimming shorts, rinsed them under the outside tap, and hung them up to dry.

'Don't you think you should put something on in case Penny comes back early?'

Hugh looked at him, as if the thought had never occurred to him. 'Maybe. Although the way she looked at some of the nude guys yesterday I'm not sure she'd mind. She didn't exactly turn into a pillar of salt, if you know what I mean.'

'She's my wife, Hugh. I'm asking you to put some clothes on.'

'All right Davey. Keep your hair on,' he said, walking into the cottage. David hated the use of the over-familiar "Davey" but he didn't rise to the bait. He liked to think he was above that sort of juvenile teasing.

Penny drove up in the hire car, and asked David to help her unload the shopping.

'Sorry darling, hurt my foot. See if Hugh can help you. And perhaps you could look at my foot later, if you wouldn't mind?'

'Of course,' she said. She called out to Hugh and he came out of his room wearing only his underpants; short white briefs that hid nothing. Penny giggled.

'See Davey, she doesn't mind.'

'What are you boys on about?' Penny asked.

'Nothing, Hugh seems to think you wouldn't object if he went around nude all the time.'

Penny laughed aloud. 'Well, maybe not in Quimper, but I've been thinking about going topless on the beach tomorrow, so why not?'

Hugh smirked at David and put his thumbs into the top of his briefs. For a moment David thought he was going to pull them off, but he didn't. 'Come on Penny, let's get the groceries unloaded,' he said, sliding into his flip-flops.

It was Hugh's turn to cook the evening meal, and David was pleased to see he'd put on a pair of shorts and a polo shirt. He lit the barbecue and waited until the coals glowed red under their coats of pale grey ash, then popped on the skewers of peppers, onions and mushrooms. Courgettes and tomatoes were set directly on the grill, along with the marinated monkfish tails. David opened the bottle of Muscadet and sipped it as the food sizzled appetizingly.

Most of the time, he did like Penny's younger colleague, and that evening he was at his most charming, complimenting Penny on her appearance, and David on his choice of wine. David knew the senior staff in Penny's firm of house builders better than the middle management staff. He played golf with the bosses, and socialized at company functions. As a senior partner in a law office, he often came in contact with building firms, but usually at a high level.

When Penny first asked him if she could invite Hugh to share their cottage for the first week of their holidays, he'd had misgivings. She explained that Hugh's wife had died of cancer, and he was bringing up their two children single-handed. She thought it would be good for him to get away for a short break, and it wouldn't intrude too much on their own holiday; they'd be moving on to a gîte in the

Auvergne on the Saturday. So rather reluctantly he had agreed. Penny was a sort of Mother Hen in the office, never having had children of her own, but no-one could ever call her soft-hearted. She was a senior accountant, and many a salesman had been rapped over the knuckles for mistakes in their paperwork. And she wasn't afraid of telling her bosses when some of their financial proposals seemed to her to veer towards the Dark Side. On the whole, David thought it was a good thing that she'd taken on Cheering Up Hugh as one of her hobbies. And certainly, apart from calling him "Davey", and the business with his underwear, Hugh had been good company.

He wondered about Penny saying she was going to go topless on the beach. She'd never shown any exhibitionist tendencies in the past. David thought she had a good figure for her age, perhaps a little sag here and there, but that was normal, he assumed. Why would she want to expose herself in public?

Whilst a lot of French women sunbathe topless, total nudity was discouraged by the locals, although they had noticed the previous day, by the rocks at the far end of the beach, a group of foreigners flouting the French conventions. Penny had actually commented on some of the men, and Hugh had joked along with her. David wondered what his reaction would be if she matched her actions to her words the next day. When she and David were getting ready for bed, he mentioned his toe, and asked her to have a look at it.

'That's odd,' she said. 'There's definitely something there. I thought you were pulling my leg earlier. Let me get my tweezers.' But the tweezers weren't able to dislodge it, so she got a sewing needle from her little repair kit, and teased the skin away from the little black dot. This time she was able to grasp it with the tweezers and pull it out. A small amount of clear plasma followed it, and she squeezed his toe until nothing more came out. She dabbed on some antiseptic cream before covering it with a plaster. The relief was instantaneous. She held up a short, sturdy black spine, but neither of them knew what it was.

'You just found it in the sand?'

'Yes. In about six inches of water. I just stood on it and the pain shot up my foot.'

'Oh well, it's out now, whatever it was.'

'Thank you darling.'

Next morning David rose early and took the plaster off his foot before he had his shower. There was no sign of infection, although the toe still looked a bit red and felt a bit tender. He drove into the village for baguettes, and Penny was up and about making the coffee when he returned. Hugh came out of his room, yawning exaggeratedly.

'Coffee's made Hugh. Join us on the terrasse when you're ready.'

David liked French breakfasts—milky coffee served in shallow bowls, chunks of bread, daubed with butter and apricot jam, sometimes buttery croissants. Hugh joined them, a towel wrapped round his middle, and Penny laughed.

'You'll have to wear a bit more than that when we have our lunch.'

'Somewhere formal, is it?'

'Not really, it's a sweet little place in Quimper. We found it last summer,' said Penny.

Hugh turned his head aside, and David guessed he must

be thinking of his wife, who had died the previous August. Then he turned back to them.

'I'm sure I'll enjoy it. And I promise to dress appropriately. But after lunch we're going to come back to the beach and join the nudists.'

The restaurant was in the centre of town, quite rustic, the tables set with simple check tablecloths, and bench seating on either side. They looked at the menu, and agreed on the plat du jour, Breton fish soup. The broth came separate, topped with slices of bread spread with the fiery, garlicky rouille, and the fish, mussels, potatoes and vegetables served as a separate course. It was delicious. David asked the waiter which fish had been used, and he said they usually made it with scorpion fish, conger eel, gurnard and weever. Sea urchin coral was stirred into the broth. As he mentioned the weever, David remembered reading about it some time before.

'Ah, that's what must have given me the sore foot,' he said. 'They bury themselves in the sand to ambush shrimp, and they have these poisonous spines that stick up. I must have stood on one.' He explained himself in his rather laboured and heavily accented French to the waiter, who sympathised, saying how painful it must have been. He said there were a lot of them off the beaches this year, because of the warmer water. David was a bit chagrined that Penny and Hugh seemed less sympathetic than the waiter. They had been knocking back the wine though, as it was David's turn to drive.

They got back to the cottage and changed for the beach. Penny and Hugh just wanted to lie and bake, too full after lunch to do more, but David went for a swim to cool off. He was very careful when wading out, to keep his eyes peeled for any sign of black spines sticking out of the sand, but he saw none. As before, the sea was very shallow for quite a distance out from the beach, but as it deepened it became noticeably cooler. He had always envied swimmers, like Penny, who had mastered the Australian crawl. He had tried to learn it, teaching himself, but it never worked out for him. After his swim he walked back up the beach and wasn't altogether surprised to find Hugh and Penny sunbathing nude.

'You don't mind darling?' Penny asked.

'Would it make any difference?' he replied.

'Of course, darling. You know I always do what you tell me.' And she laughed, as Hugh grinned beside her. David noticed the sheen of sun-tan oil on her body, and on his, wondering who had applied what to whom. He did not look at Hugh's penis. After he dried myself he put his towel in the small gap between them, and lay down beside her, obliging Hugh to move out of the way. Penny rubbed sun tan lotion on him, her hands smooth and slippery. The sun was delightfully warm, and he was so tired after his lunch, his swim and Penny's massage, that he dozed off.

When he awoke, he wasn't sure how long he had slept. Hugh and Penny were sitting together, talking quietly. Hugh had his shorts on, and Penny had pulled on her bikini bottoms, but remained topless. They both seemed very relaxed. David was still a bit groggy after his sleep, and all sorts of thoughts were going through his head. It started to get cooler, an onshore breeze blowing in from the sea, so all three headed back along the path to the cottage.

Hugh set out bread, cheese and grapes for their light supper, and he and David had some of the supermarket's cheap red wine while Penny went off for her shower.

71

'How is the family doing?' David asked.

'Great,' said Hugh. 'They've adjusted better than I thought they would, Tom in particular. He was always very close to Josie. He's in his second year, loves maths and physics. Lily wants to study music.'

'And what about you Hugh? How are you doing, truthfully?'

'Truthfully David? I still miss her lots, but it's not so painful now. In the immediate aftermath Penny, my other work colleagues, my friends, all of you, helped me so much. I'll always be grateful for that emotional support. Recently I've started to go out a bit, with other women I mean, and I no longer feel guilty about enjoying myself with them.'

As he spoke David knew, with absolute certainty, that Penny had provided more than 'emotional support'. He wondered how many of the times she'd been 'working late' or out 'visiting friends' she'd actually spent with Hugh. That's what this holiday had been about really, why she'd asked if he could join them for a week by the sea. Are they still lovers, he wondered?

Then she came outside to join the men, with a long bath towel wrapped round herself. She took a swallow of wine, loosened the towel and let it drop, standing naked before them.

Hugh slipped off his shorts and said, 'Come on David, drop them. Don't be the odd one out.'

Penny said, 'Go on David, take off your shorts. Let's all be naked this evening. Nothing hidden. Let's get everything out in the open.'

Life is funny sometimes, he thought. Under a clear blue sky, out of a clear green sea, something pierces you, and nothing will ever be the same again.

~ Into the Valley ~

THE WORD 'DUMPED' IS SOMETIMES preceded by the word 'unceremoniously', but in this case there was a ceremony of sorts. The car stopped on a long bend in the Towne Pass, and I was pulled out of the back seat. The blindfold was taken from my eyes and the cord round my ankles was cut. They frisked me again and lifted me over the roadside barrier and onto the dusty gravel slope. The heat was overpowering. All three of us were sweating up after only five minutes.

'If you live, and that's a very big if, don't try to come back, don't contact the boss, don't contact his wife. Especially don't contact his wife. Understand?'

I mumbled an answer.

'Stay off the road. We'll be watching it on the traffic cams. But you'll probably be dead by tomorrow. Be grateful we're giving you a chance. Goodbye.'

I looked around. The Panamint Mountains were many miles away; there was no chance of reaching shelter there. Behind me was the arid, gypsum-white featureless flatland stretching back to Trona and Ridgefield, where the bad guys lived. The slope ahead led down to the bottom of Death Valley, and across the other side I could see the colourful strata that marked the badlands around Zabriskie Point. I couldn't see the highest point, Manly Beacon, but I knew it was there. I needed to get there, to cross into Nevada, where I could go to ground. I knew a girl in Pahrump, Nye County, who might help me. The trouble was, the ground in between was flat, shadeless and next to impossible to cross directly. The temperature, I guessed, would be around 120 degrees. If I was going to live, and I wanted to, I needed to skirt round the central salt pans and stay on the slopes. And I'd need to walk at night. And I'd need to find water.

I sat in the shade of a Joshua Tree, next to a barrel cactus. I remembered scraps from a survival training manual. This one held water inside, and the mucilage might be unpleasant, but at least it wasn't toxic. That's a bonus here. A lot of the plants are really nasty. How to get at it though? I didn't have a knife; if I'd had one I'd have been able to cut the cords round my wrists. I kicked out with my feet until I'd scooped out a reasonable depression in the sand, and then I lay back in it. It was definitely cooler. I had shade, I was sitting in cooler sand, and I had the possibility of finding water, if my hands had been free, if I'd had a knife. Too many ifs. I picked up an angular pebble with a rough edge on it, and started rubbing at the cord.

You can feel your eyelids sweating. It's true—there's a little prickle of sweat every time you blink. I know the top of your head is an obvious place to sweat—you feel the cooling effect of evaporation as soon as a little breeze develops. You've seen Schlieren images of heat rising from a body, and you know the same kind of thing is happening to you. Your back isn't exactly pouring with sweat, but you know it's pumping out moisture to keep you cool.

Now add exercise, and it becomes much more obvious. Sweat trickles down your back and chest. Stains appear on your shirt, first between the shoulder-blades and over the breast-bone, then spreading over the whole shirt. You can almost feel it pumping out.

It's so different from the heat in Europe, where I'm from. I remember walking down the main street in Rocamadour in a heat wave, to visit the shrine of the Black Virgin. That was hot, but this is so much hotter. The heat reflects up from the ground and takes your breath away, like when you open an oven.

There's nothing obviously living here, apart from the sparse vegetation, and although you can't see it, the plants too have shut down for the day. Light is flooding in, and chemical reactions are happening, but no gases are moving in or out—not like normal plants. The breathing pores—the stomata—are shut—little green lips tightly pursed.

And what about you? The heat is a physical assault on any exposed skin. Skin that's covered is working at a rate your body has never worked at before. More sweat glands than you ever knew you had are firing a constant mist of moisture out, extracting water from your blood.

If you opened your shirt you'd see a fine sheen of sweat, a thin film of water, over your whole body surface. But opening your shirt exposes your skin to the desiccating air, and you dry out in seconds, forcing your sweat glands to remove even more water from your blood, which thickens. This forces your heart to work harder, and pushes your blood pressure up. You can feel it pounding in your chest and in your head. This makes you more anxious, so your heart pumps faster, meeting even more resistance and further increasing your blood pressure.

Eventually, if there's not enough water in your guts to be absorbed by the intestines to replenish the blood's stock, you just die.

Your heart fails, you go into anaphylactic shock, or you might get a mighty aneurism in your brain. Whatever the nature of the final catastrophe, the outcome is the same. You're another mummified heap of skin, bone and gristle in Badwater, Furnace Creek, or the dune field at Stovepipe Wells.

Not going to happen. I was so sure of that. By late afternoon I'd finally cut through the cord on my wrist. I was sweating, it's true, but I was still in the shade, and I'd dug down a little deeper into the grit. Above me, a phalanx of puffy white clouds marched across the sky, getting thicker and darker as they moved toward the far side of the valley. Was it going to rain? Was it actually going to rain? Was this going to be one of the very rare summer storms?

As the first lightning bolt lit up the underside of a cloud, the rain started, preceded by hailstones. I scrambled out of the little gully and onto a ridge, heading downhill, into the hot heart of the valley. Avoiding the road, I was cooled by the first shower, walking west, toward a patch of golden ground I recognised as the Mesquite Flat sand dunes at Stovepipe Wells. The vegetation became sparser and more woody. Mesquite trees and creosote bushes became more common. If there were any pods on the mesquites I could maybe eat them. They're in the pea family, and the seeds are edible. I sucked on a few leaves of Mormon Tea, its thirst-quenching astringency welcome, and I knew it contained a calming chemical.

The rain was now coming down very hard, and I crouched down so I wouldn't become a target for lightning. I took off all my clothes and spread them out to absorb water, wringing out my shirt into my mouth. I started laughing, started to believe I really might live through this. For a day or two after the rain stopped there would be surface water, and the plants would have sent out surface roots, absorbing this new moisture and storing it in their tissues. I estimated it would take three days to walk to Furnace

Creek, where there is a tourist hotel, with the chance of finding transport to Shoshone or Pahrump, maybe with someone heading for Las Vegas along the Red Rock Canyon road. I had money. Oh, the guys had taken my wallet and my cards, but I had a stash of bills sewn in a panel in the waistband of my pants, and they hadn't found it.

The rain lasted two hours. I watched the leaden clouds drifting over to the northern wall of the valley, in-cloud lightning flickering, until they were too far away for me to hear the thunder. The gullies ran with new streams that would dry up almost as soon as they'd started. The colours took on an intensity sharpened by moisture, plant leaves greener, red rock redder. It was really pretty, if I'd had the time to admire it, and, from my day shelter under a creosote bush, I did admire it. I also admired a little lizard under the bush, snapping up any flies or beetles which landed near him. He wasn't a very talkative companion, but that suited me fine.

Nightfall, and stars started to come out. I had never seen so many, and the numbers grew as the sky darkened. I saw the great arc of the Milky Way. There was a thin new moon, but its light was enough to keep me walking in the right direction, and the temperature was down twenty degrees or so. I wasn't worried about snakes—they'd be asleep in their burrows. Scorpions and venomous spiders might be around, but I just had to chance on not meeting any. I remembered a friend, bitten by a Brown Recluse spider, who had been ill for some months after the encounter, and it left permanent muscle damage in the arm that had been bitten. There were no dangerous big critters here. There are coyotes, but they tend to stay near the vegetated areas, like Scotty's Castle and Panamint Springs.

As the sun rose above the mountains in the east, I dug myself into the gravel again and prepared to wait out the day. I buried myself in the ground, apart from my head, which I covered with my shirt. I was close to a rainwater pool, which would probably be gone by nightfall, but I could flick my shirt over to it, and drink the water from that. I was hungry, but hunger wasn't going to be a problem. I reasoned I'd die from dehydration before starvation got me. Only I wasn't going to die.

The next night I cut across the valley floor towards Badwater, and I had a stroke of luck, coming across a hiking trail, obviously used in winter by walkers, trail bikes and ORV's. It skirted the salt pan and for a few miles it ran in parallel with the main road, which I wanted to avoid. Highway Patrol cameras scanned the road regularly, and I didn't want to picked up by them or by anyone else. The trail was easier walking, and then just as the sun was coming up I came across an emergency shelter, surrounded by litter and decorated with graffiti. Inside there was a large plastic water tank, and I drank until I was full. And then, in the dark shed, I slept on the ground. If there had been spiders or scorpions I didn't care by then.

At dusk I started walking again, realising I might make somewhere close to Furnace Creek by morning, so I could hole up for the day. The vegetation was different here, with tall *Washingtonia* palms sending their roots deep down for the hidden water. I found an abandoned house, lacking a roof, but with a cracked and derelict swimming pool. In its corner some of the rainwater remained, and I drank deeply, heedless of any germs it might contain. I made a makeshift shelter from old timbers, and lay under them while the sun roasted the pale stones around me. I used an old rusty nail to unpick the threads from my waistband, and took some money out. In the late afternoon I rose and walked on into Furnace Creek.

I was unshaven and dishevelled but I walked up to the hotel's reception desk and asked for a room. Looking at my appearance, they made me pay in advance, but that was fine. A shower and a shave later, I drank a couple of bottles of water from the minibar and went down to the restaurant for a meal. I can't remember what I ate, but I do remember how good it tasted. I had survived. I had crossed Death Valley. After my meal I walked round to the back of the hotel, near the staff quarters. A spadefoot toad hopped in front of me. I took that as a good omen. Hearing quiet Spanish voices I found a group of Mexican staff and their friends and I asked, in my halting Spanish, if they knew anyone who might be headed through Pahrump the following day. An old man with a pickup said he was going that way to get vegetables from the market. I offered him fifty dollars and he agreed to take me.

Next morning at 5am I shook hands with the old man, paid him, and we set off. By seven we were in Pahrump. It's a strange town. Either side of the main street are the licensed brothels, most displaying menus for sexual services, couched in the most flowery and euphemistic language. My friend lived on the outskirts in a trailer, and I knocked on her door.

'Come in. I'm just fixing breakfast. How have you been? Still chilling out?' she asked.

'Right, just keeping cool,' I replied.

~ Cruising ~

IT WAS DARK WHEN NUDGE woke up. It was always dark when he woke up. He swung his legs out and down, using their weight to bring his head and body up. He didn't look at the empty space in the bed to his left—training himself not to be aware of the absence. He opened the bedroom curtains just a crack to check the weather. Dry, cold, not windy. Enough information for this time of the morning. He let the curtain fall back, then pulled it tightly closed so there was no gap. That way, there was no chance of anybody outside looking in.

From force of habit he was very quiet as he washed, dressed, and made his breakfast. Porridge, coffee, toast and jam. Same as yesterday. He decided that tonight he really must wash the porridge pot properly before he went to bed. Check the clock—ten to five—high tide at quarter past six, so they'd get away early and be well out before the sun came up. What do fish do before it's light enough for them to see? Do they sleep? Sharks don't sleep, he'd read that somewhere, but what about the rest?

The skipper was already on board when Nudge got to the boat. They nodded to each other. Without being asked, he put the kettle on for a cup of tea before they sailed. It was a ritual. The other deckhand, Dumpy, arrived cursing and groaning, complaining about his hangover. Nudge didn't drink, or not very often, and he usually managed to turn down Dumpy's invitations to join him in the Volunteer. He preferred to go out and walk at night, feeling the solid unmoving ground beneath his feet. He didn't go anywhere in particular, just walked round the streets for an hour or so, another thing Agnes never understood. With her, there always had to be a reason for doing anything, a definite destination in mind. Time wasn't there just to be passed—it should be used for something constructive and meaningful.

He passed the mugs to Skip and Dumpy then sat back to drink his own tea. The engine was running sweetly, and the gear was hooked up to the winch, ready to be shot when they reached the fishing ground. There was never any rush, each of them knew what had to be done before they sailed, each just got on and did it. He rinsed the mugs and stacked them, then ran up the ladder and loosed the mooring ropes, as Skip revved the engines. Nearby, another five boats were doing the same thing. Skip liked to be first out if he could, the first boat to clear the breakwater and feel the slap of the sea. Nudge never thought about the nature of the day ahead—it would either be a good day or a bad day, and hoping for something never made it happen.

By the third good lift Skip reckoned they'd caught enough for the day, the first two covering the day's costs, and the rest making the owner's profit and their wages. No need to be greedy, leave some for tomorrow is Skip's watchword, said often enough to be boring, but not loud enough to be irritating. They headed back in the gloaming. By the time the harbour lights came in sight the boxes were packed and iced ready to be unloaded for the morning market, the gear stowed away, and the deck hosed down. Twelve hour day—nothing special.

Some nights he walked past Dumpy's house. He started doing this a couple of years ago. One Saturday afternoon he'd glanced through a narrow gap in his high garden fence and saw Dumpy's wife sunbathing topless in her garden.

He walked on, then turned around and walked back, as much to convince myself he wasn't imagining it as to see her again, although he certainly wanted to do that. By now she was lying on her back on a lounger, breasts flattened but shapely and shiny with oil, narrow waist, neat round tummy, wide hips, pale green strip of bikini cloth, and long, long legs. Dumpy's wife? How could that be? She was gorgeous, why Dumpy?

He'd gone home aroused that day, keen for sex, but Agnes had refused—the kids were out playing and could come back any minute, besides, she had too much to do. Wait till Sunday morning as usual, she'd said. So he did, but when he closed his eyes that Sunday it was Dumpy's wife he saw. And he didn't even know her name.

His walks became more regular, most nights and weekends, just round the houses. The fence gap had been mended, and he never again saw Dumpy's delicious wife, but he kept hoping. Sometimes he'd glimpse pale indistinct forms in the shadows of uncurtained rooms, sometimes he'd see silhouettes. He found one big house where the teenage daughter undressed in front of an upstairs window. He went back several nights in a row, and each time she did the same, each time a little closer, a little better illuminated by the yellow glow of the streetlight. He was almost sure she knew he was there, not to recognise him of course, but just to be aware of a dark shape standing across the road beside the bushes.

One night she stood in front of the window, naked, and pressed her body against the glass. He was mesmerised. Then her head whipped round and she jumped back, as if someone had come into the room. He should have moved away, but stupidly he stood still, long enough to see a man stare out before closing the curtain. And when he got home Agnes was in a fury. Her boss had phoned her to say he was sure he'd seen Nudge standing outside their house. She demanded to know if it was true, if this was the reason for his nocturnal walks. He denied it of course, but he was aware that his excuses sounded lame and insubstantial. A week later she moved out, taking the children.

It was a good job for him, Agnes told him, the girl's father didn't call the police. But that was one street off his route. Some nights, as he walked along the empty pavements in his quiet trainers, he imagined he was like a shark cruising among sleeping fishes.

~ A Gardener's World ~

'YOU MUST ADMIT, THIS REALLY is a bit of a golden age,' he said.

Well, there's a thing, I thought. Tim Bousfield is living in a golden age, is he? Let me count the ways. One: he's got a great job in the City, making pots of money. Two: he's got a large house in Metroland. Three: he's got lots of friends, some of whom because of One above. Four: he's got three golden-haired children, all doing *frightfully* well at school. Five: he's got a beautiful wife—Patty—the same woman I used to call Trish before he graciously took her off my hands. I'm kidding—Trish and I were never really together, except in my fantasies. But he probably *is* living in a golden age, for him anyway.

And the rest of us, his former classmates from Brookman's Park? There's not a lot golden about the age I'm living in. Some of it's maybe a sort of dirty yellow, but that's as close as it gets. Trish isn't always thrilled with her life either—she's told me so occasionally when she's overdone the poolside Pimms while I've been there doing her garden.

It was funny how we met up again, all those years after school. I run a gardening business. It's advertised as 'grounds maintenance', because that's the kind of circles I have to move in to make serious money. I lost a lot of my good customers in the financial crash—they couldn't afford my annual charges any more—so I was touting for business in the more affluent suburbs, and Trish answered the door.

'Andy? Is it really you?'

'Trish, my goodness. How are you?' I replied.

'What are you doing round here?'

'Looking for business,' I said, handing her my brochure. 'I do a lot of the gardens round here. Pools, patios, barbecues too. Basically anything outside the house that needs doing.'

'That's interesting Andy. We've got a local man who comes round twice a week, but he's no Diarmuid Gavin, just mows the lawns and weeds the borders. I'll talk to Tim tonight. You remember Tim, don't you?'

'Of course I remember Tim,' I said. 'What's he doing now?'

'Still in the City. He'll be amazed you were here. Where are you living now?

'I have a flat near the station. It's handy for the business— I work from a unit in the industrial estate next door.'

'That's great,' she said, with a noticeable lack of enthusiasm. 'I'll definitely be in touch, one way or another.'

'Thanks, Trish.'

'You know, nobody's called me Trish since schooldays. Tim calls me Patty, and now everybody else does too. Except you. You can still call me Trish.'

'Thanks, and I'm still Andy.'

So Tim took me on, and paid me handsomely. Then he and Trish decided they needed a full makeover of the garden. That was fine by me. I scoped out the garden's problem areas—a moribund rockery, a boring border, a group of unsuitable trees in the wrong place, a swimming pool without shade and nowhere to change, an overall lack of focus—and I came up with a garden design I thought might be interesting. The lawns were superb though, and very well-tended. Her local man might not be a garden designer, but he knew how to keep grass in tip-top condition.

Turned out he's a part-time greenkeeper at the golf club. Trish/Patty and I went over my ideas, and she made some eminently sensible suggestions. Then it was Chelsea, and as an RHS member I took Trish along as my guest, pointing out some things she might like. I worked out the costings and, much to my surprise, Tim agreed. He really must be loaded.

'It's going to look terrible while we're working on it, and for a couple of months afterwards, but by next Spring you'll start to love it.'

'You're very confident Andy.'

'I was well trained, Tim. I know what I'm doing.'

'Sir Charles showed me what you'd done over there, and I was very impressed. When are you able to start?'

'October. We'll do the modifications to the pool area and the rockery first, and put in the stream, waterfall and lily pond. I'll have the shrubs and the new trees containerised long before then, so we'll get them planted up next. The border will be the last thing. It'll look great next Summer.'

'Will your men need access to the house?' I knew where he was going with that question. He didn't want his trophy wife exposed to rough working men.

'No, I'll use a trailer for their equipment and tools, and we always bring a Portaloo. As long as we have access to your main gate and driveway we'll be fine. The other thing is, Tim, that this will be a construction site for a few months, and I'm going to insist that you and Patty keep away from our equipment and the working areas. I'll bring hard hats for you to use on inspection visits. Health and Safety, you know. It's all in the contract.'

'Of course. I should have thought of that.'

We signed the contract, and I continued to do the

maintenance chores in the garden over the rest of Spring and the early Summer. Sometimes Trish would come out and swim, or lounge by the pool. If she felt like talking she'd wave me over. I never took too long over these conversations; my time was limited, and I had other gardens to work on, but the odd quarter of an hour spent in her pleasant company was fine.

I'd had a huge crush on her at school, but I was excessively shy, blushing at every encounter. Meanwhile she was always running about with Tim's crowd, until the night of the school dance. Tim couldn't be there; his sister was playing in a concert, and their parents insisted he attend. And so I got to escort the lovely Trish, and she really was lovely. She was very nice to me too, making me feel at ease, dancing most of the dances with me. I was in love, instantly. When the dance finished I escorted her home, taking her hand. When we got to her door she kissed me, and I bounced all the way home. This was it!

But of course it wasn't. Next day Tim was back, and she was with him, although he did thank me for escorting her to the dance.

'Patty tells me you were an absolute gentleman.'

'Of course, as always Tim.'

And somehow I became part of his little circle of friends. That lasted until the end of school, when everyone went their separate ways. They went off to their respective universities, and I enrolled at the horticultural college, at my mother's suggestion. I soon realised it was exactly the right thing for me. I was good at it, because I loved it, being outdoors, growing things, creating landscapes. And when I finished I went to work for the council Parks Department.

Ten years gaining experience, and then I set up my own business, which has done very well, thank you.

'You never married, Andy?'

'No, I thought about a couple of times, but they never worked out.'

'I think you'd make a good husband for someone. Would you like me introduce you to some of my single friends?'

I laughed. 'Not at the moment, Trish. But I may get back to you on that.'

'I've got some married friends who like a little diversion. Would that interest you Andy?'

'Oh no, I couldn't do that.' I laughed again, and I could feel my blush spreading. Damn! That hadn't happened for years.

'Always the gentleman, Andy. You've never changed.'

'Nope. Well, must get back to work,' I said, putting my high-vis waistcoat back on. I left her lying on her lounger under the parasol on the patio, and went back to clearing out the overgrown border. It would save time the following Spring. I don't know why some women regard a single man as a challenge. I've thought about marriage a few times over the years, but not enough to want to give up my independence. At present I'm in a 'friends with benefits' relationship with a very nice young woman in the flat next door. She's divorced, bringing up two young kids on her own, and I help out with the groceries and some of her other needs. Neither of us wants to take it any further, and I know she sees other men from time to time. I even babysit for her on the occasional weekend when she wants to get away with someone.

'That's me finished for the day Trish. I'll just load the

rubbish on the trailer and head off. I'll be back next Tuesday. I was thinking ...'

'What?'

'Well, the parasols for the pool area have arrived. I can bring them next week and put them up temporarily if you like.'

'That's a great idea. Yes please.'

'Good. Young Hamish and I will bring them over and get them set up. You can have the use of them in this sunny spell before we pour concrete for the permanent supports later on.'

'We're having a barbecue on the 22nd. Would you like to come?'

'I'd love to.'

'It's starting off at 2.30.'

'I'll set up a pop-up gazebo for you in the morning, in case you need some shelter.'

'You think of everything, don't you?'

'All right if I bring a friend?'

'Your girlfriend?'

'No, my neighbour. She has two young kids, so she doesn't get out much.'

'Fine. There will be other children here, so she can bring them too.'

When I got home, there was a cuddly toy outside my neighbour's door. That was her signal that she was 'entertaining', so I waited until the following morning before phoning her.

<Hello?>

<Hi Lena, it's Andy. Do you fancy coming to a barbecue at one of my posh houses? The kids are welcome too>

<Ooh, yes Andy>

<I'll give you the details next time I see you>
<Come round tonight. I'll cook something>

I like Lena's cooking, so I took round a bottle of a rather nice Montepulciano d'Abruzzo, and after the kids were asleep we finished it between us.

My apprentice, Hamish, and I put up the big parasols and tied them off so they couldn't be moved. They'd be fine like that as long as it wasn't too windy, but they did give that all-important bit of shade by the pool. Our gazebo would provide extra cover, and somewhere for the older guests to sit. On the day of the barbecue I took over some strips of marinated beef and some pre-buttered baguettes. I like to be well prepared.

Trish's youngest girls played happily with Lena's kids, while the eldest girl, Melissa, a quiet, serious girl, helped me with the barbecue. I sort of delegated myself to cook, so I had a procession of rich neighbours coming over to refill their plates and compliment the chef. My marinated beef went down very well. Of course, I had a bundle of business cards and brochures to hand out. I noticed Tim hanging round Lena quite a bit, and she wasn't making any effort to keep him at a distance. I thought she was looking particularly attractive that day.

As the party wound down, Trish and Tim came over to thank me, Lena collected her two children, and I saw Tim slipping her a piece of paper—no doubt his private phone number.

By October I was ready to move on the garden. I excavated the lily pond and the stream course first, using the soil plus the stones from the rockery to build a mound in the north-west corner, the coolest, shadiest part, for a small clump of conifers, with shrubs and large boulders to conceal the reservoir and pump which fed a small water-fall. The return water came from the lily pond, the pipes being concealed below the stream bed. I thought it was quite an elegant design, and Trish was extremely enthusiastic. Of course the water was quite silty and scummy at first, even with the filters, but I assured her it would clear by next Spring.

The rest of the garden was a piece of cake; a pool pavilion where guests could change; a permanent gas barbecue on the patio; reshaped lawns with a pop-up sprinkler system to water them, linked to a 'grey water' reservoir so no hose-pipe ban would affect them, and some beautiful plantings in the rejuvenated border.

While all the work was going on, I occasionally noticed Tim's big Mercedes in the station car park, and Lena's cuddly toy distractor was in place these evenings. Naughty boy. When the job was completed Tim asked me to lunch with him, so we could tick off the contract completion details, and he would pay me the balance.

Lunch was very nice, and so was the cheque. Tim had that sneery look on his face, like he'd put one over on me, stolen another of my girlfriends. That's when he came away with that cheesy golden age line. Fine, I thought, he can believe what he likes, as long as keeps on contributing generously to my retirement portfolio. I suppose I could have used what I knew about his meetings with Lena to develop something with Trish, but the truth is that I didn't want to. We weren't that compatible really. I'd rather keep her as a well-connected friend in the middle of an area with some excellent business prospects. Besides, an affair with Trish would cause complications, and not just with Tim and his chequebook. It would throw my schedule right out too.

Mondays, Mrs Chalfont; alternate Tuesdays Mrs Biggs and Miss Alvanley; most Wednesdays Sir Charles' wife Monica, occasionally their daughter Claire; Thursdays my accountant's wife Gillian, Fridays Hamish's mother Effie.

I'm so glad I went into gardening. Don't believe anyone who says it's boring. The way I cultivate my flowers it's anything but.

~ Neighbours ~

THE WIFE OF THE WIFE-SWAPPERS came over one evening for a natter. I can't remember what the pretext was—it was all a long time ago—but she made it sound like it was a getting-to-know-you thing. Trouble was, I was pretty sure I didn't want to get to know her, and I seriously doubted Deirdre would want to know her partner, a busy young joiner. It was the 1970s, specifically The Year of Moustaches, and he had a bushy black one which filled his long upper lip. He was tall and rangy, smiled a lot, but I'd never found him much of a conversationalist. John, I think his name was. They had parties at the house quite often, but their house was across the road from us, and we never heard any disturbance.

I'd heard rumours about the couple, their relationship, and the things that went on at their parties, but I'd never discussed them with Deirdre. Why should I? We were happily married, with two children at school, both with good jobs, respectable. Not church-going, that would be a step too far, but as I say respectable. Wife-swapping? Extramarital sex? Other people maybe, but not us. According to the Sunday papers, the more salacious ones anyway, the ones we only read over other people's shoulders on the bus, everybody was at it, but not us. We didn't even think about it; I certainly didn't.

Our house was in the first phase of development of our site, a small estate which would eventually consist of just over a hundred dwellings. We knew the area and liked it. We were living in a council house at the time, so this would be our first 'bought house'. as they say around here. I booked the plot as soon as the sales office opened, and I watched it from the day the foundation concrete was poured until the day it was released and the key handed over to us. There were twelve families in that first phase, and we got to know most of them. We had to—there was always something that one or other of us needed, or needed to do—and we helped each other out. The closest amenities—shops, pubs, hairdresser and the like—were in the village half a mile away.

My wife and I were very much in love—still are, for that matter—and our two girls attended the local primary school. School hours were regular and predictable, and in those days pupils didn't have the 3-page menu of extracurricular activities they have now, so it was easy to make arrangements for Deirdre to drop them off before she went to work, and to pick them up afterwards. She taught at a different primary school, but her hours were similar. Most of the families in that first phase had young children, so we led similar lives. A few had older children at secondary school, and their challenges were slightly different from ours, but we got on well.

That was the thing; our social life was pretty good. Three or four couples, including us, would go into the city for meals together—there were no restaurants nearby. And the Spar grocer was very limited, so we often saw our friends in the large supermarket in the nearby town at weekends. A few times that first year we had parties in each other's houses. Even while new houses continued to be built and occupied, we First Families were close. Deirdre had her favourite friends, and I did too.

I picked elderberries in the Autumn, and by January my elderberry wine was ready to be launched. I took a bottle to a party, and the host poured us a glass each of his wine and my wine. After tasting mine, he poured the contents of his whole bottle down the sink. That surprised me, but in a good way. It felt even better later, when I danced with his wife. She was petite, vivacious, on her second marriage, and she'd been a dancer. Have you ever been in a situation where, by accident, you discover your perfect, ideal, responsive dancing partner, and she is not your wife, and you are not her husband? It scared the living daylights out of me. We did not dance again that night; in fact it took years for me to let myself go on a dance floor again, to release my inner boogie-man.

The next party was at our place. Six couples that night, with Deirdre surpassing herself on the food, and me circulating with wine—white, red and elder. The couple from the cul-de-sac were there. Brenda was a red-head, her husband Mark had black curly hair. They had two kids—one of each variety—and their idea of bringing them up seemed to consist of consulting them and negotiating with them about everything, as though their opinions were of equal value to those of the grown-ups. Not my way of child-rearing; I expect they found it in a book. Don't get me wrong, I love my children, but I'm an adult, with experience and knowledge which they haven't yet acquired. I will support them, try to advise and guide them, but they are not my 'friends' nor my 'best buddies'. I am their loving but resolute father.

I have slobbish tendencies. I'm not a total slob, but I could get close to it on some occasions, especially in the early years of our marriage. For instance, when I got home from work I used to hang my jacket on a peg in the cupboard under the stairs, take off my tie, close the cupboard door and go through to the kitchen-dining room for one of Deirdre's very tasty meals. I didn't bother to wash my hands before I ate, because I don't eat with my fingers, so what would be the point? I'm different now, but that's what I was like then.

The last phase of building, probably about a year after the builders started, was across the road from us, where the site huts had been. It was a terraced row of two-storey houses, with narrow frontages. The curtains in one of the houses always seemed to be closed. The couple never socialised with the rest of us, and to honest I can't remember the husband at all. The wife was an attractive blonde. I knew her name, and we had spoken a few times. Then my friend Donald brought her along to a book club I belonged to. She only came to one meeting, although I looked for her at every meeting after that. But Donald confided in me some weeks later that his work colleague, my neighbour, was a secret nudist, hence the closed curtains. The turnover of houses was quite fast, however, and the couple sold up and moved away with their small child after six months. The house next door to them was the one where the alleged swappers lived.

I'm pretty sure now that Lynn, the swappee, came over that evening to sound us out on the possibility of swapping, but seeing us together, hearing us talking about ourselves and our children, she realised that the lifestyle didn't hold any appeal for us. I don't think she learned any more about us then or later, but we didn't have much to do with them for the remainder of their time on the estate. Us? We stayed more than twenty years, losing touch with all of the original householders, until new neighbours through the wall and their very loud parties made us move.

Oh yes, that Saturday party at our house? It was good, plenty of food, plenty to drink, no dancing, because we didn't have much room, and our two girls were sleeping upstairs. But it broke up about eleven, and everyone drifted back to their own homes.

On the Sunday morning Brenda came over to our place. She was very sheepish, wouldn't meet our eyes. She handed me my wallet, said she'd found it in our driveway. Then she went home. We couldn't understand it; my wallet had been in my jacket pocket, in the cupboard under the stairs. How could it have got outside? I checked it over; the money was still there. This was before credit cards were widely used, but I had things like my driving licence, photos of Deirdre and the girls, personal stuff.

In the afternoon Mark rang the doorbell and told us the truth. Brenda had gone into the cupboard, fished through my jacket pockets, and taken my wallet. He said she was ashamed and embarrassed, and so was he. She'd never done anything like this before. He blamed it on the drink. I suppose we could have called the police, made it official, but we didn't.

We never spoke to either of them again, and I decided to leave the elderberries for the blackbirds next year.

~ Power ~

THERE WAS ALWAYS A HUM. When it rained, or when there was low cloud or mist, the hum seemed louder, with an underlying buzz like the sound of bees in the apple trees in Spring. Roseanne was sure it wasn't just sound that came out of the wires. There must surely be something else, something that caused Toby's frequent colds, Ruth's bad moods, Amy's funny turns and her headaches. Simon, of course, noticed nothing, downplayed her concerns, but then he always sailed through life smiling, didn't he? Bastard. She did love him, but he infuriated her sometimes. She wondered if other couples were like that.

They had lived in the house under the power line for three years, bought it when the estate was just being built. The sales lady hadn't drawn their attention to the overhead wires, but they'd walked all the way through the building site on their second visit, and noticed the pylons and the suspended cables, passing directly over the place where the foundations of their house were being laid. They'd asked about it, and been assured there was no risk. The builders had even sent a document which explained in some detail the extensive research undertaken into the risks of living below power lines, and summarised that there was no statistical evidence for any human health problems for those who lived under the wires.

Simon, of course, was satisfied with the explanation. He always was. A word from an authoritative sounding source, anyone higher up the food web from himself, and he swallows it all. Roseanne is not so easily taken in. The world is full of bullshit, she thinks, and she gets frustrated when she feels the wool is being pulled over her eyes. The trouble is she doesn't usually know enough facts to refute things. Sometimes she wishes she'd been a scientist instead of a music teacher, but her physics teacher had such terrible BO that she dropped the subject as soon as she could. The music teacher was a tyrant, but at least she smelled nice. And Roseanne found that playing clarinet took her places: to the school orchestra, to small ensembles with like-minded friends, to being in demand. It opened up her social life, and gave her confidence.

The first year they were in the house, which was a very nice modern family home, on the largish side but affordable, everything seemed normal. Simon worked as a telephone engineer, based in Edinburgh, but serving the whole of the Lothians. Roseanne was a peripatetic music teacher in West Lothian, teaching woodwind instruments, which actually covered a wide range of instruments from piccolos to bassoons. She also did private tutoring on clarinet and saxophone.

What with all of that, Simon's frequent call-outs to repair telecoms equipment, juggling three young children and their curricular and extra-curricular activities, Roseanne was often exhausted by the time meals, baths and bedtime stories were over. Only she couldn't get to sleep with that constant damned hum.

'Roseanne,' she said to herself, 'Why don't you have a little hot toddy to help you to the Land of Nod?'

'Sounds good to me,' she replied to herself.

And that was probably how it started. The hot toddies became a nightly thing until she dispensed with the hot water, the honey and the lemon, and just drank the whisky. She told herself it was OK, that lots of people had a relaxing drink in the quiet of an evening, but she realised, even at that early stage, that it wasn't altogether A Good Thing, that it wasn't without its dangers.

Nobody noticed. She was sure of that. Simon definitely didn't notice. He was absent so much, even when he was there, that he'd miss a herd of charging wildebeest if they came through the living room. Unless they kicked his computer. He'd notice that, and probably ask Roseanne to shoo them away. Toby wouldn't notice; he was like his father in so many ways, clumsy, uncoordinated, geeky. And yet he was such a sweet boy, thoughtful and caring about his mother and his sisters. He didn't understand his father, but sons never do, do they?

Amy's too absorbed in her animals. She always wanted a dog, but we told her it wouldn't be fair, with all of us so busy, and away from the house so much. We have a cat—Tinny—short for Tinnitus, and Amy's mad about her, but I think the cat resents Amy constantly wanting to stroke her. She's an outdoor cat, black with white paws. She tolerates Amy, but she's quite aloof with the rest of us. We open the door in the morning to let her out, whatever the weather, and she stays out until hunger or the need for warmth or shelter brings her back at nights. I don't think she goes after birds, at least I haven't noticed her paying them any attention, but I know she catches voles and mice, so that's OK. I think Amy might have ambitions to become a vet when she grows up, but that's a long way off—she's only nine.

Ruth is our oldest, at sixteen. She's a problem at times. She never used to be; she had a happy nature when she was little. Some time later, she changed. She clammed up, wouldn't speak to us for days on end. I suspected something might have happened on her thirteenth birthday, but she wouldn't ever speak about it. Most of the time she's fine, but she has these dark days when she goes about with a face like thunder. 'Boyfriend trouble?' I asked her one time.

'No,' she replied furiously, and stormed off to her room. She didn't come out until the next morning. I thought it best to leave her to deal with her problems in her own way. Maybe I should have tried harder, but there were times when I just didn't have the energy.

I think Toby might have inherited my musical genes, but he has his father's semi-detached attitudes as well, so he can't settle on anything for very long. He started to learn clarinet when he was eleven, but he wouldn't practise. He preferred going out with his pals. He gave up playing after six months. It was a pity, because I thought he showed promise. If he'd been one of my paid pupils I'd have persuaded him to stick in, maybe through the parents. Parental guilt is a great motivator, I always think. But you can't use that when it's your own son, can you? I'm guilty enough already.

I've tried not to nag Simon too much about the power line, because it's not his fault, and there's nothing he can do about it. Maybe in a couple of years we'll think about moving house, taking a step up the property ladder, but we can't quite afford it just yet. And sometimes living here is actually quite nice.

I remember one day last winter. We were lying in bed, after our usual Sunday morning lovemaking, no sound from the kids, but the hum from the wires was particularly loud. Still naked, I pulled back the curtains and saw that a thick mist had come down overnight. The house, the garden, the whole neighbourhood was shrouded, and I couldn't see the trees in the country park at the back of the house.

'Fancy a quick walk before breakfast?' I asked.

'Sure,' said Simon, 'A little break before the chaos.' We dressed quickly, put on our rain gear, and slipped out of the house, walking down the path to the park. We crossed the stream over the stone footbridge and walked up the steep track on the other side.

The mist deadened all the sound in the trees, and we couldn't see the tops of them. Suddenly, out of the murk, we heard an unearthly sound, a kind of hooted conversation with several voices at the same time, coming from the mist above our heads. I heard wingbeats among the honks and hoots. Whooper swans, I thought, arriving from Russia or Scandinavia. It was a magical experience. I hoped they'd miss the power lines. I know some lines have spinning disks—diverters—so that swans can avoid them, but in this mist they wouldn't be able to see them.

We walked home, and the Sunday morning breakfast pandemonium started. This month Amy was a vegan. Ruth wasn't; she wanted bacon, eggs and beans. Amy said if I cooked that she was going to her room because the smell of bacon and eggs frying made her feel sick. Simon suggested that I cook some pancakes, as if that was some kind of compromise solution. Toby helped himself to some cereal, smelled the milk and said it was off. It wasn't completely off, just heading that way, so I decided I would use it up to make pancakes. My father always made pancakes with sour milk. The extra acidity reacts with the baking powder to make them lighter, he said. So that's the way I make my fluffy American-style pancakes, and the kids love them. It was almost funny, Simon suggesting the right thing by accident.

Ruth's crisis came just before her exams, as these things often do. She'd been particularly moody for a few days, and we put it down to stress. She'd gone out with some of her friends one evening.

'Remember to be back by ten, darling,' I said.

She almost snarled at me. 'I know. You don't have to remind me.' And she was off.

She came in just before nine and went straight to her room. I didn't think anything of it. Amy was watching something about animals on the television, Toby was playing computer games online with some of his nerdy friends, and Simon was away on a training course. I sat for a while with my whisky, then decided it was bedtime for the kids. Amy and Toby were fine with it, but when I looked for Ruth she wasn't in her room. I thought she might be having a shower, but she wasn't in the bathroom. I wasn't worried then, just maybe in need of a second whisky. I searched the rest of the house in an increasing state of anxiety, but there was no sign of her.

Then I noticed the back door was unlocked. I went outside, but the rain was chucking down, so I went back in for my umbrella and a torch, although I didn't really think she'd be in the garden. But she was. She was standing directly under the power line, face turned up to let the rain wash over her, her hair lank and saturated behind her.

'Ruth, what are you doing? What's the matter?'

'I thought some of the electricity might leak out and kill me,' she sobbed. 'But it hasn't.'

'Why would you want it to do that Ruth?'

'Because it's over, my life is over. Denise said she doesn't love me, she loves Alice.'

'What do you mean Ruth?'

'What do you think, mother? What do you actually think?'

~ Totems ~

CHARLES WAS THINKING ABOUT totems again. The train was passing by the same landmarks it always did, but he wasn't taking them in, his thoughts idly drifting back to memories of his days at St Andrews all those years ago. On a whim he'd taken an anthropology module in his first year, although his main degree was in economics. He'd gone on to do an MBA at Strathclyde before starting a career in banking, but sometimes, when his brain was in neutral, his thoughts turned again to his studies of human societies. What would it be like, he thought, to live like that? It wasn't that he was going to rush off to the Amazon rainforest and talk to the Yanomami, but he was fascinated by the idea of people feeling strong connections to the places they lived in and the creatures around them. Perhaps some of the earliest Scottish tribes might have called themselves Bear people, or Wolf people, or Lynx people? He thought of the animal carvings on the standing stones in Aberdeenshire.

What would his totem animal be? His spirit bird was Raven, that was relatively easy to decide on. But he always had problems thinking what his spirit *animal* would be. The usual ones didn't really appeal to him. In some ways he was attracted to Bear, but he thought in reality they'd be a bit unsavoury, certainly unfriendly, probably a bit whiffy. He didn't trust wolves, and Lynx was an unknown quantity—big shy pussycats maybe?

The trouble was, although he'd seen them all on telly, he hadn't come across them in real life, unlike Raven. Walking in the hills as he used to, he had often seen ravens, looking down on him and calling with that deep *pruk-pruk* sound, or tumbling from the crags above him for the sheer joy of it. No, the choice of animal was the problem. He could be Seal, often found swimming in the harbour in North Berwick, where his family sometimes holidayed when he was young. He rejected Whale and Dolphin as he felt no connection to them.

His Chinese astrological character, his birth sign, was Horse. He didn't believe in astrology, not at all, but Horse *was* worth thinking about. There were horses in the field next door to his granny when he was a boy, and he often talked to them. He didn't know if they ever listened, but it gave him pleasure to think there was some kind of communication going on.

As the train drew in to his station, he seemed to have decided on Raven and Horse. They would be his signifiers, his totems. A totem is much stronger than a talisman; it's an aspect of personality, embedded in one's character. He believed he had elements of raven-ness and of horse-ness in him. He considered the intelligence of ravens, their curiosity, their farsightedness, their playfulness. That was him sometimes. He thought about the endless patience of the horse, their unflappability, their abiding silent strength. That was him too, or sometimes it was.

Walking from the train station through the suburban streets to his home, he recalled a black and white film about the Kwakiutl, from the Pacific Northwest. They were in very large canoes, and in the prow of each stood a man wearing an animal mask and costume. Bear, Wolf and Eagle led the rowers round the headland to the shore, where they danced. The totem poles showed these creatures, as well as 'Thunderbird', Salmon, Orca and others. Thunderbird was mythic—the bird which summons thunder—but the others were real creatures. The film stayed in his mind for many years. He'd like to have seen one of these ceremonies; a real one, not one just performed for tourists.

Arriving home, he took off his jacket and hung it in the wardrobe—ravens take care of their plumage—and washed his hands in the *en suite* bathroom before coming downstairs to see what Desiree had cooked for them—she was usually home before him, as her office was in North London. Philip and Louise, their teenagers, had finished their homework, and were lounging in front of the fire, talking quietly. They don't always talk quietly, so that was quite pleasant. Desiree came through from the kitchen and joined Charles on the sofa, giving him a quick kiss.

'I want to ask you something, Desi.'

'Yes Charles?'

'If you could think of a bird and a mammal you can identify with, what would they be?'

'Why would I want to do that?'

'Humour me please. Which bird sums you up? A robin?'

'No, that's too soppy. A great tit?'

'Desi!' he said, looking over at the children. She had a wicked twinkle in her eye.

'Sorry. All right. I'll be serious. I quite like owls. Remember I bought that barn owl painting for Philip's room?'

'Oh yes, that's a good one. And a mammal?'

'A goat, a nanny-goat.'

'I don't think you're goaty at all. Think of another one.'

'A fox,' she said, and Charles knew instantly that was the right answer. She's a fox, sly, cunning, single-minded, fearless, he thought. He knew Fox, from having seen them many times in countryside walks. As long as people don't have dogs with them they're a lot less shy than you might expect.

Charles thought about Owl. Familiar birds, the screech of courting tawnies on winter nights, a pale barn owl floating over a misty Aberdeenshire hayfield at twilight, a short-eared owl hunting in daylight, flying a search pattern over a Perthshire moor. Owl was right for Desiree, wide-eyed, alert, senses heightened, a night creature. He loved his Owl-woman, his Fox-woman.

'Well Charles, you've animalised me. What are you?'

'Can you guess Desiree?'

'Aye-aye,' she said without hesitation.

'Aye-aye?'

'Yup, definitely.'

'Why?'

'You're always pointing that long bony finger. You point it at me, you point it at the children. I bet you point it at your colleagues in the bank. I bet it annoys them too.'

'Actually, it's Horse,' he said. She snorted.

'The one that comes last in every race? The one that pulls Benny Hill's milk cart?

'The horse is a noble animal,' he said. She snorted again. 'It is. Horse is calm, strong, willing.'

'They eat grass and oats; they roll around in mud, they let people sit on their backs. What's noble about that?'

'There's just something about them I like. Gorgeous creatures.'

'They're used for hunting foxes, darling. Have you thought about that? Imagine those great lumbering brutes and packs of baying hounds chasing down little old me?

Think about those mad red-coated bastards with their little tin trumpets, urging their horses on.'

'Pink,' Charles said.

'Pink? What are you talking about?'

'Their coats. It's called 'hunting pink', that colour.'

'Don't quibble Charles, and stop pointing your aye-aye finger at me. Go and poke about for some grubs. Whooo-hoooh!'

'That's what male owls do. Females reply with "Kee-wik". Or they simply screech.'

'Aye-aye, Sir, I stand corrected. Oh, by the way Charles, I'm going to be late home tomorrow night. I need to go over the papers for my New York trip again. Can you be home by six and make the children their supper?'

'Of course,' he replied. They lived in Hatfield and both worked in London, although Charles had started off working in a bank in his native Scotland. Desiree had to go over to New York every couple of months for her work. She was a corporate lawyer in a practice that had international connections. She didn't mind it, and Charles had become used to it. She liked New York. She'd been to lots of places for her firm, to Rome, Tokyo, and recently Beijing, but New York was her favourite. At first it was sort of glamorous for her, and she'd come back from her trips very excited, telling Charles and the children about all the things she'd seen, and the places she'd visited. But in the last couple of years it had settled into a routine for her, and she didn't talk much about the city, although she could and did enjoy going to other places on family holidays. This time she was set to travel on the Friday, then work in the firm's apartment over the weekend and be fresh for her Monday morning meeting. She'd normally have meetings from Monday to Wednesday or Thursday, then fly home on Friday. Oh, the exotic life of the international jet-set lawyer.

It wouldn't have suited Charles. He liked his job in the bank, plodding along in the Business Development arm, assessing start-ups and expanding companies in the agribusiness sector. He knew it well, having worked there for fifteen years. His colleagues in the technologies, commodities and manufacturing sectors took a bit of a pounding from time to time—market forces and all—but farming doesn't change quickly, and he was less stressed than most. Solid, good old dependable Charles, an absolute workhorse, that was him.

There didn't seem to be anything special about this New York trip, but when she chatted with him online she said she was being called to a meeting of the senior partners in London on the following Tuesday.

<Don't know if it'll be good news or bad news. Rumours are that there's to be some restructuring. Things a bit sticky here today, hope tomorrow goes better. Off out to lunch. Love you. Kee-wik. x>

And Charles replied: *<Relax, you'll be fine. Woo-hoo. xxx>*

She arrived home on the Friday evening. She was well used to the time difference by now, and she didn't suffer from jet-lag very often, but she was obviously thinking about her upcoming meeting and went to bed early. The weekend was taken up with the children, as usual, Charles taking Philip to his fencing class, while Desi and Louise headed off to dance school. On the Sunday she said she couldn't settle, so they all piled in to the Beemer and headed off to a carvery for Sunday lunch. Monday evening she said the rumour mill was working overtime about the restructuring, with some saying the firm had been sold to an American law office, while others said they were going to expand into China and the Far East after the Brexit vote. Charles had had an uncomfortable day at the bank, also because of Brexit. He had been asked to draw up a strategy for the agri-business finance sector if European farming subsidies weren't replaced in full by British subsidies. That was the scenario he predicted would happen, trying to be as far sighted as a raven.

He kept his head down and started crunching the numbers, and the outcome didn't look too rosy for his own career. However, he had cultivated connections in other sectors, particularly in IT, and he decided to make use of them—packing his parachute as it were, in case it was needed. They were both feeling a bit apprehensive and down at suppertime on the Monday, and later they sat with their laptops in their separate halves of the study.

Next day the time for Desiree's meeting came and went, and there was no word from her, and none at lunch-time or in the afternoon. Charles was beginning to think they were headed for a double disaster as he walked up the road from the station, but Desiree greeted him with a warm smile, a kiss, and a glass of champagne.

'It's under an embargo until next week darling, but it's tremendous news. I'm to be a senior partner from next month.'

'Wonderful,' he replied, drawing her in for a hug and a champagney kiss. 'What about the restructuring?'

'I'll tell you after supper, when the kids are in their rooms. I don't want to say anything in front of them, in case they say something to their friends. If this leaks it could affect the company shares. Now finish your champagne and put the glasses away. We'll have the rest later.'

It was a happy meal. Philip and Louise could tell something was up, but Desiree didn't say anything. Philip went upstairs to do his homework and to revise for his exams, while Louise cleared the table and started the dishwasher. As soon as she was safely out of the way Desiree and Charles sat on the sofa with their champagne.

'Well then,' he asked, 'What about the restructuring?'

'There will be some, but it's not too much, and it's actually very sensible. We're pulling out of South America and cutting back in Africa, but these were never my areas. China and Japan are being handled by a new spin-off associate in Beijing, and North America will stay much the same. Australia and New Zealand are ramping up. In Europe we'll concentrate on France, Germany and Italy, but the Brussels office will close.'

'And what about your own position?'

'Mostly growing the UK business and dealing with our bigger corporate clients. It'll be a huge jump in salary, and I'm getting stock options as a bonus. We'll be rich darling. You can give up your job if you like.'

'No chance. My job may change too, but I'll tell you about that later. So, no more travelling?'

'I'll still have to do some, but a lot less, and mostly in the UK.'

'No more New York trips?'

'No. My New York associate, Ethan, is going to be promoted, and one of my juniors will be doing the routine liaison work with him. He doesn't know yet, and I can't tell him.'

'You'll miss New York,' Charles said.

'Yes, I will. I'll miss using the company apartment, getting up early to jog in Central Park, going downstairs to buy bagels and coffee for breakfast and taking them upstairs to my office. I'll miss the galleries, especially MOMA, and the concerts. Yes, I'll miss my little vixen's den in the city.'

'And you'll miss the restaurants, the bars, the night life, your little *tête-à-têtes* in the apartment with Ethan.'

She gasped and drew back. 'You know?'

'I know.'

'How long have you known?'

'From the start.'

'How did you find out?'

'Ethan told me.'

'Ethan?'

'Yes. He phoned me one evening—afternoon his time— as you were flying back home. I think it would have been your second or third trip, and the first time he'd slept with you.'

'That would be the third trip. Why did he tell you? Did he say?'

'Wanted to confess, apologise maybe. He told me he'd been showing you around after client meetings during the day, taking you to restaurants, the best bars, a couple of night clubs. He'd taken you to a bar where there was dancing, and you had danced together. Then you'd both gone back to the apartment. He was very sorry, said it was just a friendship between two close colleagues that went a bit too far. It shouldn't have happened, but you'd both just got caught up in the moment.'

'That was true. What did you say?'

'I thanked him for letting me know. He seemed to be

genuinely sorry. I told him I understood, but I didn't know what I was going to do.'

'You've known for three years, but you didn't say anything to me?'

'No. It didn't make any difference to the way you treated me. Ethan said you'd talked about me, said how much you loved me. We talked after most of your visits that first year. He said you didn't love him, and there was no chance you'd leave me for him. I think he was sad about that, but he's a realist; he accepted it.'

'I can't believe you said nothing to me.'

'I knew it wouldn't last. Either the firm would move you or you'd lose interest in him. You know me Desiree; I think things through. I weigh up the alternatives. I love you too much to lose you. I know how much a divorce would hurt us and the children, how much it would damage our lives and our careers. Like the old cart horse that I am, I just stood still and waited.' He paused. 'It's finished, isn't it?'

'Yes. We haven't slept together this year, and that's been three trips. And before you ask, Charles, there's never been anybody else. I do love you, and I was terrified you'd find out. I never wanted to hurt you.'

'Oh, it hurt at first, but you were happy in your work, you had a companion who took you places, helped you find your feet in a new world. He made you happy, Desi. I can't feel hurt by that, because that's what I want too.'

'If it had been the other way around, and you'd slept with someone else, I'd have killed you. I would have been so jealous.'

'I know. I've seen foxes fighting.'

'I'd have scratched your eyes out, and then bitten your head off with my pointy little teeth.'

'Good job I've never done it then.'

'Never been tempted?'

'That's different, but it's never been difficult for me to say no.'

'I'm switching to whisky, Charles, champagne isn't working for me tonight. Would you like one?'

She poured the drinks and Charles stood up, clinked her glass and sipped his whisky, feeling its warmth spread through him. She hugged him and kissed him deeply, with tears in her eyes.

'I'm not sure I know you Charles. I'm not even sure I've *ever* known you. You've surprised me so much tonight. You're not an aye-aye after all. You really *are* a dark horse— calm, strong, deep.'

'I like to think so.'

She smiled at him.

~ Produce ~

'GOT ANY ICE CREAM, Antonio?' the big man asked.
The smaller teenager gave an embarrassed laugh.
'Just potatoes. And it's Jimmy.'

'Thought you were Italian, Antonio.'

'No, no, as Scottish as you.'

'Now, just because we're in Scotland and I speak with a Scottish accent, doesn't mean I'm Scottish. I could have been born somewhere else, couldn't I, Antonio?'

'It's Jimmy. Scottish name. Born in Edinburgh.'

'Your father Italian, Antonio old boy?'

'No. From Paisley.'

'You look Italian. Got the hair, the eyes, the skin. Good chip shop in Paisley. You know it?'

'No. Never been there.'

'Well, I can't stand here discussing ice cream all day, Antonio. Move your fucking potatoes so I can get the pizzas re-stocked. Mid-morning, need to shift them.'

Not for the first time Jimmy wished he didn't have to work here in the mini-market, especially in Fresh Produce. Everything was either heavy—the potatoes, the onions, the cabbages, or fragile—strawberries, peaches, pears. But still, at least he wasn't in Meat, like that horrible bully. Actually, he was lucky to get this weekend job. The manager was a neighbour and a family friend. The wages weren't much, but they'd help him when he left school in a year's time.

But there was definitely something troubling about these latest jibes from Big Dave. Do I really look Italian? he thought. Mum and Dad don't look Italian, but I've got the dark curly hair, the dark eyes. Where did they come from? Do I have some distant Italian relatives I don't know about? He thought about asking his mother, but something told him this might not be a good idea. What if they confess they're not my real parents? He put the thoughts to one side for the time being.

Three weeks later his parents said they were going out for a meal, and asked him to babysit his younger sister. Jimmy didn't mind. Madelaine was easy to get on with, and his parents seldom went out together on their own. Family outings were much more the norm.

Maddie was up in her room doing her homework, and Jimmy sat for a long time thinking about the physical differences between himself and his parents. Madeleine was clearly her father's daughter. She had Dad's fair skin and freckles, his height, his red hair. She looked as if she was developing a similar body shape to her mum. But what about himself? Could he have been adopted? There had never been any discussion along those lines, but he knew adoptions were sometimes concealed. His mother kept official documents, the car's registration, the deeds of the house, the medical records and other stuff in a box in the hall cupboard. Almost certainly his birth certificate or adoption papers would be there.

Quietly he slipped upstairs and opened the hall cupboard. There was a box, as he'd remembered, and he started going through the collection of brown envelopes. He opened the marriage certificate first, noting the date of the marriage, which was the date he knew his parents celebrated their anniversary, and the year he expected it to be, three years before his birth. Then he opened his own birth certificate and read it for the first time. He gasped with shock when he saw that the column for Father's Name had been left blank. What did that mean? And how could he ever ask his parents about it?

As it happened, the opportunity to do just that came up the following week. Jimmy's father, Stuart, kept fit by playing badminton with friends every Tuesday evening in the local sports centre. His usual partner called off that week, and he offered to take Jimmy along as a substitute.

'I won't be very good, Dad.'

'That's all right. I don't usually play to win, just to have a bit of fun. You remember how to play, don't you?'

'Sure, but it's been a while.'

So the two of went out after a light tea and played a doubles match, which they lost. Then Stuart played a mixed doubles with his usual female partner, a woman who worked beside Jimmy's mum. Jimmy watched the match, and saw how good his dad was at the game, how he anticipated his opponents' moves, how he reached to his full height before smashing the shuttlecock over the net. The woman, whose name was Beth, offered to give Jimmy a singles game. She was closer to Jimmy's height, so the match wasn't quite as one-sided, but she still beat him. He thanked her for the game, then went off to the locker room to shower and change with his father.

He had never seen his father naked, but there, standing next to each other, he looked at them both in the locker room mirror. His dad looked too.

'How come we don't look alike, Dad?' he asked.

His father reddened visibly, a flush spreading up from his upper chest to his neck, and then to his cheeks.

'There's something I need to tell you, son. I always planned on telling you when you were eighteen, but I guess

I should tell you earlier. Your Mum's going shopping on Thursday night. I'll tell you everything then. Please don't mention anything to your mother. OK?'

'Of course Dad.'

'What I will say now is that I love you, and I'm proud of you. You're a good son.' He almost sobbed as he said the last sentence. They finished dressing and went out to the car. His Dad hugged him.

Jimmy found it difficult to sleep that night, although he knew he was closer to knowing the truth about his origins. It was obvious to him that his dad might not be his biological father, although then and now he was still 'Dad'.

Next evening, his mum said she and Madeleine were going shopping at the mall on Thursday. 'So you boys will have to entertain yourselves.'

'Fine Mhairi. We'll maybe play computer games. That's something Jimmy can beat me at, so he can get even with me for the badminton.'

'Good idea, Dad,' Jimmy said, smiling.

When Thursday rolled around, Mum and Madeleine drove off to the mall. They were going to meet up with Beth and her daughter, then go shopping for clothes for the girls. 'Maddie's growing up so fast, Stuart, she needs a whole new wardrobe.'

When they were alone Stuart motioned Jimmy through to the kitchen, and they sat on opposite sides of the small table.

'Your mother didn't want you ever to know this, so you mustn't let on that you know. Can you promise me that Jimmy?'

'I promise Dad,' said Jimmy.

'The first thing I need to tell you is that you've probably worked out that I'm not your biological father.' Jimmy nodded.

'But you're my son, always have been, always will be. Nothing will ever change that.'

'I know Dad.'

'That's the most important thing. You, Maddie and your mum, are everything to me. I'd do anything for you.' Jimmy nodded again.

'This is very hard for me, son. Give me a minute.' He paused.

'When I first met your mum, I had left Paisley Grammar, and I was studying civil engineering at Paisley Tech., before it became a University. I met your mum at a Students' Union dance. She was an apprentice hairdresser. We just looked at each other and that was it. We danced together all that evening. I don't think we even drank anything. Afterwards I walked her home, and she brought me in to meet her parents. I was very shy with them, but they seemed to like me. I said goodnight to them, and I asked Mhairi to go out with me for a coffee the following night. She said yes, and I arranged to pick her up.

I went round about seven the following night, and her dad told me just to go upstairs to her room. She had some religious pictures on the walls, and a couple of framed photographs on her bedside cabinet. I picked one of them up while she was getting her coat on. It was a boy, around her age or slightly older. She got embarrassed when she noticed, and took the photo out of my hand. I asked her who it was. An old boyfriend, she said.

I never saw that photo in her room again.

I graduated, and we'd been going steady for more than a

year, when I asked her to marry me. I had an offer of a job with a firm in Edinburgh, and in those days housing was cheap, so we rented a small flat in Stockbridge, got married and moved in.

We were very happy together. We didn't want to start a family right away, so we stuck to the rhythm method, as your mum was still a practicing Catholic. You know all about the rhythm method, don't you Jimmy? Although I suspect you've been using condoms?' Jimmy didn't reply.

'Things were great for a couple of years, and then she suddenly became moody, a bit sad. I thought she was maybe depressed about something, but I didn't know what was wrong. She had a good job in a very classy salon, and my job was great, so we had no money worries. Then things fell apart. One night she said she had to work late at the salon. I didn't believe her, because she'd never worked late on a week night before, so I went there. It was closed, of course. She came home, quite late, and I confronted her. She confessed. Her old boyfriend had found out from her parents where she was living, and he'd contacted her. They'd been having an affair for two months, and she'd just discovered she was pregnant. She didn't know which of us was the father. I insisted she break it off with him immediately. I phoned her parents, and they were devastated by Mhairi's behaviour, and their own involvement. They demanded she break it off immediately, or they would disown her. So she did. She was very worried all through the pregnancy. She'd go through phases of being certain it was mine, and then phases when she had doubts.

Then you were born, and it was obvious who the father was. I'd thought he was Italian, from that fleeting glimpse of her old photograph, but he was actually half-Spanish—

Scottish father, Spanish mother. Your mother went to pieces. She couldn't cope with anything, so I was both father and mother to you in those first few weeks. Maybe that's why we've always got on so well with each other. I wanted to put my name on your birth certificate, but she said that would be a lie and a sin, and insisted the father's name was left blank. We moved back to Paisley for a month, so your Gran could look after her. I loved you from the start, Jimmy. You need to know that.'

'I do know that Dad.' They were both crying.

'Your mother said you must never know, that you would think badly of her, but I think I always knew this day would come. I hope you don't think less of her, now that you know. She's a wonderful wife to me, and a wonderful mother to you and Maddie.'

'Thanks for telling me Dad. And don't worry, I'll keep my promise.'

The next Saturday, in the back room of the mini-market, Jimmy was putting trays of onions and peppers on to his trolley, when Dave came over.

'Hey Antonio, fancy one of my pizzas?'

'It's Jaime,' said Jimmy, 'And it's Spanish, not Italian.' He skewered a red onion with his packaging cutter, and smacked it into Dave's hand. 'Smell that and cry, fat boy.'

~ Droplets ~

IT HAD RAINED DURING the night. Droplets of water
hung on the wires of the rotary clothes drier like dew on
a spider's web. And just like that the memory came back, of
walking along the path in the woods on a glorious autumn
morning, the mist lifting off the meadow and floating up
through the trees, dew glistening on long grass stems by
the side of the path. In the distance Jim heard the constant
hum of traffic from the highway, the occasional rasping
roar of a motorbike engine revving up through the gears.
Here, closer to him, a blackbird's alarm call, the raucous
calling of rooks in the trees, the 'chack' of jackdaws and the
thin 'tseep-tseep' of a blue-tit foraging in the bushes. Jim
was on his own. He preferred, then, to rise early and leave
his wife sleeping, closing the door quietly, but never quietly enough that she didn't hear it, and to walk up the Sunday morning street to the country park boundary. There
was no boundary fence. The houses stopped, and an open
meadow led down to the stream, the old bridge, and the
track into the trees.

Ten years. Ten years since he'd left the place and tried to
forget it, but then something daft like droplets on a clothes
drier brought it all back, the path through the trees, the
faraway traffic, the brassiere hanging from a bush, close to
the stream bank on the far side of the park. Of course he'd
been curious, taking the steep path he knew so well down
to the old mine workings, the gallery pierced by openings
to let light into the levels cut by the old shale miners, the
levels that led off into the darkness. And a little way in, a
white shape on the ground showed faintly. He crept closer,

until he saw the body of a naked girl. He called out to her, his voice deadened by the low roof of the mine, but there was no response.

He could not bring himself to come any closer, but turned and came out into the autumn sunshine. It was warmer now, and he found himself running, gasping, as he headed for the phone box in the centre of the village, since this was before mobile phones were in general use.

He phoned Mary first to tell her what had happened, then dialled 999 and waited by the phone box until the police arrived; two cars and an incident van. He led them through the park to the mine.

Naturally they were suspicious of him at first—he didn't even resent that. 'How did you know the mine workings were there?' And he told them about his interest in geology, seeing fossil plants in the shale beds in the Cannel Water, and following the seam to the old workings, which he'd explored as far as he dared, finding deep water at the ends of some of the mine openings, and conscious of the weight of soil, rock and trees above his head. He told them he thought the gallery had been used recently by locals, pointing to the remains of fires, empty beer cans and a couple of syringes.

Two of the policemen, one uniformed, one CID, escorted him home, to where Mary was becoming frantic. The detective interviewed her in the kitchen, while Jim sat with the other policeman in the living room. Then Mary came through to the living room, while the detective spoke to him again.

'I think we've just about finished here, Mr Lassiter, but would you mind if we had a quick look round your house and garden? I don't want to go through the formality of getting a warrant if I don't have to, but you can ask me to get one if you'd prefer that.'

'No, go ahead,' said Jim.

The two policemen did their 'quick look round' and came back to him.

'Thanks very much Mr Lassiter. We will probably want to get in touch with you this coming week. I know you teach at St Anthony's, so it will be an evening visit.'

They left, and Mary came to sit beside him. He put his arms round her and she started to cry.

'What's wrong?' he said. 'It's over.'

'It's not over Jim, it's not. I just feel horrible, having to answer all these questions about you, your walks in the wood, our relationship, the company you keep, and thinking about that girl lying dead in the darkness. I don't know if I'll ever get over that.'

'You know I didn't do anything Mary. Tell me you believe me.'

'I don't think you did, Jim, but this whole business has got me thinking all kinds of thoughts.'

'About me?' I asked.

'Yes... No... I don't want to think any more. I'm going to bed.'

Jim sat with a glass of whisky in his hand. He tried to drink it, but it didn't taste good. He poured it down the sink and went to bed. Mary was asleep, and he noticed she'd taken one of her herbal sleeping tablets. Some time during the night he woke, feeling Mary's body shift. She seemed to be sobbing, and then she settled.

Jim woke next morning feeling disoriented, although he'd had neither whisky nor a sleeping pill. Mary was in a deep sleep, and he didn't have the heart to wake her. As usual he had his cereal and coffee on his own, and then drove off to St Anthony's, and his job as a science teacher. In his first class, some of the pupils seemed rather distracted, and Julia, the brightest pupil in my class, glanced at him, flushed, and glanced away.

At the break, he found the reason. The local radio had mentioned the discovery of a girl's body 'by an amateur geologist' in the woods. Enough of the pupils and staff had heard it and put two and two together to start the rumour mill grinding away. The head teacher came into the staff room and sought Jim out. 'Was it you who found the girl?'

'Yes, it was. Should I say anything to my classes?'

'No, I don't think you should Jim. If you can get through today without mentioning it, I'd be grateful. I think you should take the rest of the week off on compassionate grounds, and I'll get a supply teacher in. I'll make an announcement at assembly tomorrow. Would that be OK?'

'What will you say?'

'Just that you're taking leave of absence for the rest of the week.'

'Thanks George, that would be for the best. I'm hoping the police will clear it up very quickly and things will go back to normal. It's been very upsetting for Mary and I.'

'I can see it must be,' he said.

He finished the day on autopilot, aware of the stares of the pupils and the questioning glances of his fellow teachers. He didn't feel like talking about it, and in any case he thought that the police might prefer that he said nothing. When he got home there was a note from Mary on the kitchen table. She had phoned in sick and was meeting up with her friend Louise.

On the Wednesday the detective phoned and asked if he

and Mary would be in that evening. Their investigations were nearly complete, and he wanted to bring them up to date. They sat uncomfortably in the living room, while the Inspector briefed them.

'Basically, it was a drug overdose. The girl was sixteen, and she had become a prostitute to feed her habit. We don't know if she had a bad batch of drugs or not—we're waiting for forensics to confirm—but the mines were a regular hang-out for her and her friends. She sometimes slept there on an old mattress. Her family knew what she was doing; they basically couldn't control her. We've questioned her friends, but we think it was just a tragic accident. We'll make an announcement to the press tomorrow.'

'So I'm not under suspicion?' Jim asked.

'No sir, we are sorry for the inconvenience, and we understand how upset you both must be, but we have your statements, and I'm almost certain the matter is now closed as far as we are concerned. Thank you both for your co-operation.'

'Can I say something, Inspector?' said Mary. 'You are right about it being upsetting, and I'm relieved it's over for Jim, but I've been having nightmares ever since, and what you've told us tonight doesn't really make it any better. While you were speaking I had a vision of that poor girl, alone and dying in the dark, under the ground. I don't know if I'll ever be able to get it out of my head.'

'I understand, Mrs Lassiter. I'll ask our Liaison Officer to make an appointment with you. She'll be able to recommend a specialist who could talk to you.'

'I'm grateful,' said Mary, as she showed the Inspector out.

Mary had four counselling sessions and she'd also been

seeing more of her friend Louise. Jim thought she was getting over the shock of the event, so it was a considerable surprise when he came home from work one day and Mary asked him to take a seat at the kitchen table.

'Jim, I'm very sorry, but I'm leaving, and I want a divorce.'

'A divorce? Why? I'm willing to think about us moving away to somewhere new, but why a divorce?'

'I'm moving in with Louise. I'm sorry, but I just can't stay here with you. I hope we can be ...' She paused.

'Friends?' Jim said. 'Of course we can be friends. I still love you.'

'I've given in my notice. I start my new job in a month.'

'So that's the deadline, is it?' he asked.

'It is. 20th of December.'

'Just before Christmas.'

'Don't, Jim, please don't.'

'All right, I'll try to be civilised about it.'

And he was. At home they skirted round each other. Jim moved into the guestroom. And then she was packing up her things. The removal van drove up on the 18th of December, loaded her clothes and the furniture she wanted to take, and drove away. She kissed him tenderly, and got into her car with tears in her eyes, and that was it.

Although the house was owned jointly, Jim had been the one paying the mortgage, but he quickly realised the house was too big and too expensive for one person living alone, so he put it on the market and it sold quickly. He moved into a rented flat and began to go out more, but he found it difficult to socialise with women of his own age, and he didn't want to use a dating service. Strangely, it was his star pupil Julia, now in her final year, and with a very bright future ahead of her, who helped make the change in his life. Jim had met her mother Diana on previous parents' nights, but when she came along to the last one to talk about Julia's future at university, she impressed him tremendously. She was attractive, lively, widowed, and bringing up Julia on her own in a house close to the school. Julia noticed the looks Jim was giving her mother, and smirked at him.

'Go on, Mr Lassiter, ask Mum out. You know you want to.'

'Julia, please...' He paused, and looked at her mother's smiling face. 'Would you like to come out with me on Saturday, Mrs Alston?'

'It's Diana, Jim, and yes, I'd love to. Come round for supper.'

And he did. Jim never went back to the mines, but not long after the girl's death the old workings had been bricked up and closed off forever. Health and Safety, they said, Health and Safety.

Diana and Jim were married later that year, on the 18th of December. Julia was the beautiful bridesmaid. Jim had invited Mary and Louise, but they didn't reply to his invitation.

~ Last Fall ~

A COLD EVENING, BUT THE FIRE burned brightly, and Josh had laid by a good pile of logs to keep it going through the night. The smoke smelled almost sweet—good cedar wood. The fire was so bright that he could see nothing behind it. He rolled out of his shelter and stood up. Three paces beyond the blaze he stopped to look at the sky. There was still a hint of blue in it, and towards the horizon it shaded from burnt orange to brown. The first stars were beginning to shine. One planet—he didn't know which one—shone the brightest. It was too early for moonrise, and the crags and forest were invisible. He turned back to the shelter and sat there with his back against his pack and his feet in the sleeping bag. He took a swig of Scotch from his hip flask and finished his coffee. He was starting to think about tomorrow's trek, but he dozed off—he couldn't help himself. He was wakened by a tugging at his shoulder.

Mid-October is sort of up against the limits for wilderness hiking in Oregon, but the fall colours peak about then, and the snows don't usually arrive until later in the month. He had set off from Eugene and followed the road into the park, and hired a cabin for five nights, although he was only planning to hike for three days. He filed his itinerary and cell phone number with the park office, and told them he'd be back by Thursday night at the latest. He was a member of the Portland club, and said he'd been hiking the Mount Hood Park the previous year, so they knew he was experienced. His emergency contact was an ex-neighbour, a hiking buddy who couldn't get away this year. One of the rangers knew him, so that was fine too.

The first day was wonderful. The trail was well-marked and easy, and he managed twelve miles before setting up camp in a clearing near one of the beautiful lakes. He suspended his food from a high tree branch, well away from the tarp, and he made sure there were no food smells near his sleeping area. There were bears around—he'd seen scat a couple of times (bears do just what folk say they do in the woods). Josh had never had problems with bears in the past, and nothing else in this park would be likely to give him any concerns. So, relaxed, tired and well-enough fed, he turned in to his sleeping bag under the shelter, and slept until a cool morning breeze woke him just as the sky was getting light.

He loved being out here on his own. It gave him time to think about his life without distractions. Over coffee he started to go over in his mind the problem he'd found insurmountable back home: what to do about his son Tom's persistent truancy and poor performance at school. The underlying cause was the separation, obviously, and his resentment of his mother's new partner. His daughter Melissa had adjusted much better to the new living arrangements, but then she'd always been closer to her mother. When Claire told him she'd been seeing someone else and had fallen in love with him, he thought he was doing the right thing by moving out and giving her her freedom, but while he saw the children regularly, Tom was obviously not coping well. Josh's mother was furious with him for not, as she put it, fighting for his family, but he didn't see it that way. He didn't own Claire; she was a free human being, as he was, and could make her own choices, to go, to return, to make her own way in life, or to share it with him.

Whatever happened, they were heading for a family conference to try to sort things out. He'd had very little to do with Wilson, Claire's new partner, until now, but he figured that would have to change. And there was no way he could have Tom move in with him—he was living in a rented one-room apartment, and couldn't afford anything else.

Setting out, he decided he would move off-trail and loop round behind a small lake with a rocky outcrop behind it. The going was tougher, obviously, but he had a good map and a GPS unit, so he wasn't worried about getting lost. He made the lake by mid-morning and climbed halfway up the outcrop so he could look out over the valley. Lower down the slope by the edge of the meadow he saw the outline of what appeared to be a bear. Getting out his field glasses he saw it was a female, and she had a good-sized cub with her. They were gorging on manzanita berries, mouthing down and stripping the berries from twigs between the crimson leaves of the shrubs. Suddenly the mother stopped, rose on her hind legs and sniffed the air, staring in Josh's direction. He didn't think she'd be too worried by his presence—he was far enough away from her not to be a threat. But something had spooked her.

Then he heard the chop-chop-chop sound a bear makes when it rapidly opens and closes its mouth in a display of aggression. The sound came from above him, and as he turned to look up he saw a big male bear quite close by, on the top of his little crag. The bear was focussed on the mother and cub below, so Josh quietly moved off, taking out the canister of pepper spray from his pack, and slowly walking back the way he had come. He got back to his overnight bivouac site and walked back onto the made trail. A morning gone, but nothing was lost, just time. That was a frightening experience, but it was quite something to have witnessed it. As he moved off down the trail he wondered what the outcome would be, but he had no way of knowing.

His second day's walk was shorter than the first, so he'd have to make up ground on the third day to get back to the campsite and his cabin. He strung his tarp on a line between two trees, before collecting cedar logs for a fire. After his bear encounter he decided he'd try to keep the fire going through the night, or for as long as he could. But after his meal and his coffee, he dozed off until he felt the movement against his shoulder.

Sometimes, waking up, Josh needed to convince himself he was no longer sleeping, no longer in the confused state of dreaming. Images flashed through his mind—a bear, a thief, his father—but as he turned his head groggily these visions vanished. He could see nothing, and he heard nothing but the rising wind. The edge of the tarp had come loose, and the corner was flapping against him. He took up a manzanita branch and dropped it into the embers of the fire. The leaves and twigs spat and crackled, sending out a pleasant scent. He put on some more of yesterday's dry cedar logs, and was rewarded by the first fingers of flame.

The sky was completely black now, stars obscured by cloud, and he wondered if it would rain. Sure enough, it did, but the tarp, newly secured, kept him dry, and the fire, although it spat when raindrops hit, was warm and comforting.

He set off at first light, with an eighteen mile hike ahead of him, but it was easy walking. A couple of miles out he caught a bad smell, and looked for the source. Surrounded by flies, he found the corpse of a bear cub, its haunches partly eaten. He trekked on into the afternoon, becoming weary but not wanting to rest. Nearing evening he came towards the campground and saw a car parked near his cabin. There were three figures sitting at a picnic table. Getting closer, the woman stood up, said something to the children, and waved to him. Josh waved back, recognising Claire, Melissa and Tom. There was no sign of Wilson. For the first time in months, he began to smile.

~ Think Bike! ~

I'M ALWAYS BUYING THINGS ON impulse. I don't normally discuss these purchases with Emily in advance, but they're usually small things, and she doesn't get too upset when I walk in with a couple of new shirts, a bottle of good wine, or a dozen oysters reduced for quick sale. We talk about the really big things though, like a house, or a grand piano. I knew I couldn't just go out and buy a motorbike on impulse. It was something we'd have to discuss and agree on. We don't actually have a grand piano. We do have a nice house though, a small bungalow. We downsized when I retired, made sure it was too small to accommodate overnight visits from our children and their families. We're not stupid.

I'd been a biker in my thirties, drove a small Honda to and from work, in the days before I married, had kids and needed to take Eddie and Frieda to school every morning. You can't get three on a motor bike, so I sold it, learned to drive a car and did my share of chauffeuring. Emily and I liked to drive out in the country too, while the kids fought in the back seat or died of boredom. I used to drive a lot of the roads I'd ridden along on my motorbike, and that brought back happy memories.

There's something about a bright summer day that says, 'Good day for a run.' And I know just what that voice means, that little voice at the back of my pensioner's skull. That voice spoke from the memory of rides along the road beside Loch Lubnaig, or the long pull up Glen Ogle, with a Hercules transport plane on low level manoeuvres flying 500 feet above the road.

There was another voice, a quieter, shyer voice, reminding me of the dangers of bikes. I'd had the usual small mishaps, and then one serious accident, when I broke my collar bone. But I've seen some bad ones. Driving the car once, I saw a biker on the road after a collision, his feet shuddering in a fit, the awful sound of Cheyne-Stokes breathing. *Kidney Donor Weather*, the little voice said, that first break of good weather in spring when boys and their toys take to the roads. It tried to remind me about driving to work in gale force crosswinds, horizontal rain in your face, snow, or skittering along on a sheet of winter ice.

But the happy voice was stronger. 'Nothing will happen to you,' I said to myself. 'You can look after yourself. It'll be a final fling, before you're too old.' I went to work on Emily, playing the nostalgia card, looking wistfully at bikes and bikers, so she knew what I was thinking. She didn't put up any objections, not once. I began to think she might be OK with it.

'I don't think we need two cars any more Emily.'

'But sometimes we do. Sometimes you go into town, and I need to go to the supermarket, or out with my friends. We *do* need two.'

'It costs us a fortune, running two cars. Let's think about alternatives,' I suggested.

'All right, we'll do that,' she said.

She changed the subject, but I didn't stop thinking about it. I started looking in motorbike showrooms. I didn't want a Harley Davidson, never liked them. I didn't want a BMW, or a big fancy 1000cc monster. I found a 500cc Honda that I liked. The only thing was, it cost over £5k, and that would be a big chunk out of our savings. I couldn't really justify the cost to Emily. I mean she was very frugal on behalf of both of us. Our big spend every year was on our holiday, which I've never grudged.

We usually go on Saga tours. Neither of us like the thought of cruises, but Saga's fine. You know what they say SAGA stands for? Sex Annually, Generally August. I still think that's funny. I love Italy: Tuscany, Rome, the Lakes, Venice. Gorgeous places, and we both love the food and the ambiance. Emily and I always enjoy the company on these tours, but with me the friendships end after the holidays. Emily likes to keep in touch with some of them, and I'm pleased that she does. She exchanges postcards, emails and occasionally texts with a few of these holiday friends, and I've often heard her laughing at some of the emails she gets. Because we go to Italy so often I'm learning the language too, getting ready for the next trip. There's a guy in my Italian class, a few years older than me, and he's a Born Again Biker. There's a lot of them about. That's the crowd I'd be joining.

That's not a good thought. I don't want to be a born again anything, trying to recapture a lost youth when I didn't much like it the first time round. I'd rather grow old with Emily. And I can't get out of my head the memory of my own accident, and seeing that other poor bloody biker lying twitching on the road. Realistically, I know I'm too old to control a powerful modern motorbike. So, very reluctantly, I started to come to terms with the fact that I wasn't going to buy one.

And then Emily surprised me one night. 'I've been thinking about alternative transport,' she said.

'That's good,' I replied. What have you decided?'

'I've bought a bicycle. It's in the shed. Come and have a look.'

I was amazed when I saw it, a white and shiny road bike, with dropped handlebars and very narrow tyres. I picked it up.

'It's so light, Emily. You'll be able to go really fast on it. But I'm not sure it'll be very practical for shopping trips.'

'Of course not, silly. I'll use the car for shopping. You can use your bus pass if you need to go into town, or the big car if I'm not using it. We'll give Frieda the small car—she needs one for her work. So we'll be a one car family from now on, and I'll be able to get fit.'

And so she did. Within a few months she was wearing lycra shorts and a tank top over a sports bra. Most weekends, rain or shine, she was out on the road, clocking up the miles. She joined our local cycling club, and went on runs with them. She looked ten years younger, and her energy levels were way up. I couldn't have been happier for her.

I was getting used to public transport, and it wasn't too bad, apart from the fact that I couldn't stay in town too late or I'd miss the last bus home. So I started going out to my local pubs more often. It didn't do my waistline any good, but you're only old once. Then one night, after I'd been out and had a few beers, Emily glanced up from her laptop, where I presumed she'd been working on her emails.

'Archie?' she asked.

'I'm all ears,' I replied.

'No, that's Dumbo,' she said. I thought that was quite a witty remark of hers. 'Listen Archie. Remember Anne from the Venice trip?'

'Oh yes. Very nice woman, a bit younger than us, wasn't she?'

'Younger than you, darling, but not so much younger

than me.' I got the feeling I should have kept my mouth shut.

'She's got a two for one offer on a short Mediterranean cruise that's leaving in a fortnight. One of those last-minute deals. And she wants me to come with her.'

'Oh, that'd be nice for you. Won't you miss your cycling?' I asked.

'It's only nine days. And they've got a gym and a swimming pool on board. I'll still be able to keep fit.'

That was that. The next week was a bit of a flurry of activity, Emily shopping for cruise-appropriate clothing, getting currency, arranging for transport to Southampton and so on.

While she was away she sent me emails, often with photos of the cruise stops—Barcelona, Majorca, Malta, Naples and so on. The selfies showed Emily after a make-over in the beauty salon. She looked great. Then Anne outside the same salon. She looked great too. Then Anne and Emily by the pool. I didn't recognise Emily's bikini, but it was very flattering. Anne and Emily in restaurants. Emily and Anne at the ship's disco, both looking a little flushed. The photos for the rest of the week were all similar, apart from the city scenes. Mostly it was just the two of them, but one was of Anne with a tanned and fit young man. The caption read: *Anne's toy-boy.* I looked again at the one in the disco. I recognised Anne's boyfriend in the melee, but there was another man in the background, quite close to Emily. He seemed very familiar. I racked my brains, trying to recall where I'd seen him, and then the penny dropped. Lonesome George, once of Emily's friends from the cycling group. They called him that because he was single, having divorced a few years ago, but the name was a joke, because he was always with a woman, different women all the time.

Then, on the last day of the holiday, from the airport north of Rome, when the girls were about to fly home, came an email from Anne, addressed to Emily and cc-ed to me. The attached photos started off very similar to the ones Emily had sent me, but there were a lot of new ones. Emily and George at the pool, Emily and George in the bar, her arm round his waist, Emily and George on the dance floor, smooching to a slow number, and the last one showing Emily and George in a ship's cabin. Emily was naked, sitting on George's lap and kissing him, on a bed which showed evident signs of recent use.

A second email came in, very soon after the first. There was no content, but in the subject line was a single word: *Oops!*

~ The balloon ~

THE LITTLE GIRL IS WALKING ALONG the street, clutching a string. Floating above her head is a helium-filled balloon—pink and heart-shaped, for Valentine's Day.

She is wearing a red coat, a striking foil to her curly blond hair. Her eyes are blue-grey and seem to be always moving, always open, scanning. She takes in her surroundings very carefully, and looks people—even strangers—straight in the eye. It can be disconcerting to some, but she is unaware of that. Her expression is almost always serious. It makes her appear much more mature than would be normal for a seven-year-old.

She is holding the hand of her father, who has access rights at weekends. In the morning they had visited a museum—which she liked enormously, especially the stuffed animals. Afterwards he took her to a McDonald's, where he had given her the balloon. He called her his Valentine Girl. She ate all her burger, carefully wiping her lips with a new serviette after each mouthful. She did not have any ketchup, as she did not want to make her face messy. She only managed a few of her fries, but she insisted her father finish the remainder in addition to his own meal. Her mother had an obsession with not wasting food, and had passed it on to her daughter.

It is raining when they leave the restaurant, cold, and the streets are wet, dull and crowded. They are on their way to a cinema, for an afternoon show. At a busy zebra crossing, her balloon string is snagged by a woman's umbrella. Her father laughs and reaches up to disentangle it. In the process, the end of the string somehow slips out of her hand, and the balloon sails up above the traffic, bright and shiny against the grey sky. It is soon lost to view, twirling and bobbing in the February gusts.

She is too angry to cry. That balloon had been hers, her very own, and now it is lost. It is not her fault it has blown away—she blames her father. He should have paid more attention, been more careful with her possessions. The sense of loss, and the anger at her father, remains with her in the cinema. Later, telling her mother about her day, she says she cannot even remember whether or not she had enjoyed the film. Later still, she will punish her father by refusing to go with him on his next scheduled visit. She does not notice his sad, pained expression, and she ignores the new balloon he holds out to her.

I could say that was when a bitch was born, but that wouldn't be true. I'm sure the potential was there already, but perhaps the incident reinforced that potential. Still, I don't think any of us could have foreseen how she would turn out twenty years later, the strong and independent-minded editor of a woman's fashion magazine.

She was good at her job. That probably goes without saying. She knew what she wanted, and how to get it; usually by surrounding herself with 'can do' subordinates. The magazine owners were delighted with her; circulation was rising steadily. She wasn't an innovator, not really, but she knew an opportunity when it was presented to her. I hope you're not getting the impression that she was unpleasant to her staff, because she wasn't, or at least not intentionally. She just kind of fixed them with a stare from those intense blue-grey eyes, framed by hair that was still blond, but no longer curly. She got the performances out of them.

How do I know all this? I am her father, or rather her

male parent, as her mother left me when Linette was five. At the time there wasn't another man; she just felt she had outgrown me, or I had outlived my usefulness to her, or something in between. Louise was several years older than me, and much more experienced, but I was besotted. I thought she liked my youthful energy and enthusiasm—I was in my mid-twenties when we married, starting a new career as a journalist. Sadly, for me anyway. at the end of the day I was superfluous to her requirements. And it seemed, after a few years, that I was superfluous to Linette's needs too.

Luckily for me, I eventually found someone else to share my city centre flat. By then Louise had her sugar daddy second husband, and since his income was much higher than mine, I petitioned the court to reduce her spousal allowance, although I knew I couldn't get out of paying child support for Linette. After looking at our incomes and outgoings, the judge said that it appeared she should be paying me an allowance. This seriously annoyed her, so our two lawyers went into a huddle and came up with an ingenious solution, which we, and the court, accepted. Sugar Daddy would legally adopt Linette and become responsible for her support—he wasn't a bad man, just rich and powerful, and he seemed genuinely fond of the girl. Neither Louise nor I had to pay the other anything. We had already split the income from the sale of the house, after she moved into Sugar Daddy's much larger town house, so I was legally free and clear of financial commitments. Naomi and I were able to marry.

Louise and I seemed to get on a lot better than we did when we were married, and we agreed we would get together informally at least once a month, so she could keep me updated about Linette. And although the formal visitation schedule had been dropped, Linette and I did get together from time to time. I had met Gerald a few times, and discovered I rather liked him. He was much more Louise's type than I ever was. We should never have married, but love is blind, as the saying goes, and I had loved her, but I never felt as comfortable with her as I did with Naomi. And so sometimes I met up with Louise, and sometimes with Gerald, and it was all rather amicable, after such a difficult start.

I kept a watching brief on Linette's development, through the difficult teenage years, and then through business school. She and I met up at times too. When Louise and Gerald wanted an exotic holiday on their own, Naomi and I looked after Linette. In turn, Linette helped with our two children, Thomas and Elsie. And I gave Linette the occasional birthday treat, as long as Louise didn't have anything planned. Naomi and Louise were never actually very close, but Naomi said she respected my ex; there was never any animosity on either side.

When Linette graduated, Gerald was able to get her a job in a magazine he'd invested in, but after that it was down to her own talents to stay afloat or to sink and drown. As it happened she rose up, rather inexorably, because she was damn good at her job. She moved through the corporate levels with surprising suddenness, and also with a surprising lack of resentment from those she overtook. They recognised her skills and her single-mindedness. I think, too, that they were rather scared of her determination to succeed, an ambition so strong it left no room for anything else, for friendship, for affection, for love. They knew they could never be like that, and I think some of the women felt sorry for her.

In time Linette was made editor, and for some years things went well for her, and for the magazine. Circulation rose, as she introduced new features, new styles, new formats, all of which seemed to be popular with her readership. But then things stalled; circulation plateaued, and profits declined as costs continued to rise.

She might have been a bully, but an unconventional one. She had such a strength of purpose, such single-mindedness, such a conviction in the rightness of her thoughts, and such a focus on her own goals, that anyone or anything which got in her way was just brushed aside as irrelevant and far too trivial to be worthy of her consideration. She didn't mean to be nasty; it was simply a by-product of her character. She believed that she must be listened to, because it was her that was doing the talking.

There was a problem. Her magazine's proprietors no longer liked her—she either patronised or hectored them— and when she was being conciliatory her insincerity was obvious. More worrying to them was that circulation was falling, and audience research indicated an increasing reader dissatisfaction with the magazine—a feeling of staleness. New features, insisted on by the owners, were introduced, but were never given adequate publicity or prominence. After a few issues they were dropped, equally informally. She always insisted these failures were due to inherent weaknesses in the ideas themselves—she dismissed them as half-baked or gimmicky. The money men believed that some of them would have worked, attracting more readers, if they had been pursued more vigorously. A collision was looming, but Linette ignored the signs.

Her sacking was inevitable. Amid a flurry of publicity, a rising young star of the fashion industry, a young man who ticked all the boxes for communication skills, good looks and social inclusiveness, was parachuted in. Linette agreed to work alongside him for three months, in exchange for a substantial golden handshake. Then at the end of that time she took her personal belongings down to the underground car park. I had been tipped off by one of her colleagues, and I was waiting by her car.

I stepped forward, holding out a pink, heart-shaped balloon, for it was Valentine's Day. She looked into my eyes, smiled, kissed me and said, 'Not for me Dad. Take it home for your other girl.' And that's what I did.

~ The name game ~

Unconsciously the red-head scratched her bare arm, the bright green nail polish lightly skimming over her freckled skin with its fine blonde hairs. She pursed her lips and frowned at the phone held in her other hand.

What would her name be, I wondered? Something with vowels in it? Flora, Natasha, Linda maybe? I've always associated red-heads with soft-sounding names. Dark-haired girls have more consonants; blondes short, monosyllabic names, or shortened names, punchy, bright. That's my theory anyway.

The previous month, a bright day in early Spring when I was heading for town, I saw a girl sitting outside the station, smoking. She seemed nervous, excited, I don't know, certainly ill at ease. She smoked aggressively, blowing the smoke away from her as hard as she could. An impartial observer, me. I bought my ticket and went outside to the platform. The girl walked past me, listening to her smartphone through earbuds. A young man shouted a name. Level with me, I saw her blush, her eyes flicking from side to side, but she kept on walking. Then he came after her, calling her name again, 'Catherine! Catherine!' She kept on walking, as if she didn't hear him. He started to run after her, taking her arm. 'Why did you walk away? Why did you walk away?'

Of course, I couldn't hear her reply. I saw her lips moving as they both walked behind a group of fellow passengers waiting for the same train. My attention was momentarily caught by a young father holding the hand of a little girl. I think it's nice, that today's young men are involved so much in looking after their children. It didn't happen like that when I was young. It was the man's job to go out to work and earn enough to support the family, and the woman's job to look after the home and bring up the children.

I don't know about families from personal experience, never having been married. And being brought up in a council care home kind of sets you apart from social norms anyway. I was a strong, healthy lad, growing up, and well-built withal, so I didn't have any real problems with the abuse thing, unlike so many of my contemporaries. And for some reason I had a reputation for violence—entirely undeserved in my view. It was only ever retaliation, and always thoroughly deserved.

What was Catherine up to? Or maybe it was Katherine, or Kathryn, or some other variation. I think I'll catalogue her as a Katherine, not Kath, for that would make her blonde. But the hard K is brunette. These days though, with so many women dyeing their hair, it's hard to tell what their original colour was. I don't like blue hair, it looks wishy-washy, neither one thing nor another, and the original hair colour always shines through. I rather like reddish highlights in brown hair, quite subtle that.

Back to Katherine. She obviously wanted to dump her boyfriend, but wasn't quite sure how she intended doing it. Walking away made it clear she didn't want to face him. She was nervous, but sure of her decision, and she didn't want to get into a fight or an argument. I can understand that. Arguments are pointless. If you don't want to do something, you don't have to; you just sort it out. You don't have to carry a weapon to get your point across. For a guy like me, tall, well set up, there are several ways of avoiding disagreements. I think my favourite is to put a hand on a shoulder, and just press down. Subliminal messages are exchanged and understood, without voices having to be raised. No means no.

Women have different ways of dealing with situations. I like observing women, trying to figure out their motives and strategies. I'm not weird; I think a lot of men are like me. Doesn't mean we're stalkers, or pervs, just that we like women, their differences from us men. Bit of a social anthropologist, me, or at least a student of human nature.

I see Katherine becoming increasing bored and dissatisfied with her relationship with... let's call him Tony. He looked like a Tony. He's possessive and jealous; a real control freak. So what if Katherine does want to go out dancing, get a better job, move back to Partick—somebody has to. That was a joke. I didn't hear her speak, just him, which is how I knew her name, and he spoke standard Western Scotland, educated sub-class. 'Why did you walk away?' is educated. 'Wherr d'ye hink ye're gaun?' would have been the norm for someone like me a few years ago—*was* the norm in fact. Maybe 'Wherr d'ye hink ye're gaun, *hen*?' Forthright, but with an underlying affection—hen.

Green nails is a psychiatric social worker retained by the Council to provide background reports for the courts and the social work teams. Dr L Watson is her name, hence my idle curiosity about her first name.

'Just let me put the meeting date on your case file, Mr George, and I'll be right with you.' She fiddled with her phone for a few more minutes. When did everyone become so techie? It's all phones these days. However did we manage without them? Whatever happened to paper notebooks, printed diaries? I know she was recording our interview on her phone.

'Thanks for being so patient, Mr George. Last week you had started telling me about the incident at the bus stop in Bath Street. That was when the young mother called the policeman over and he had to caution you over your behaviour.'

'He didn't *have to* caution me, Dr Watson. He *chose* to. There's a difference. He could have just told me to move along, and I'd have done it. He could have told the woman it wasn't worth making a fuss about it, maybe I'd had too much to drink or something? That would have defused the situation. But he didn't. She told him what I'd said to her and her child, and he immediately took her side and started going through the formal procedures, logging the complaint, getting names and addresses and taking down the details. The little boy was just smirking at me the whole time, obnoxious little twat. He was at the centre of it all, Mr Big Man, everything revolving around him. Manipulative wee swine.'

'His mother said you called him a horrible little boy, a four-eyed fiend, and that you berated her for letting him get away with it.'

'That's where it all starts to go wrong, Dr Watson, when the mothers take the easy way out and give in to the vile behaviour of their brats. Do you know I once heard a young middle-class mother saying she would have to give her little girl a red card for misbehaving. A *Red Card*? I ask you, for a seven-year old? A thump round the head would put a stop to it quickly enough. It worked for me in the home. If I was ever out of line, a quick wallop taught me right from wrong. And nothing said about it afterwards.

Instant punishment, instant learning. Bad parents are the problem. Weak parents. Children are malleable; you know that from your training, Dr Watson, surely?'

She didn't answer that one, and that didn't surprise me. These professionals; they're so circumspect. That's another word I wouldn't have used when I was younger. That's what comes of going to adult classes. You learn the right word to describe what happens when a psycho-whatever avoids talking about herself. She's not the focus for this little verbal waltz, I am, so she turned it back to me.

'Are you saying violence would have solved her problem, Mr George?'

'Not necessarily, Dr Watson. Perhaps things had gone too far for his behaviour to have been controlled. And in any case I wouldn't have called it 'violence'. Physical correction would be a more appropriate term. But a better strategy would have been to control his manipulative behaviour by not acceding to his bullying, don't you think?'

'And you know all about bullying, don't you? From being brought up in a care home, don't you? Don't you think your behaviour was bullying, Mr George?'

I sighed. 'Somewhere on the bullying spectrum perhaps, Dr Watson. But I meant well, I do assure you.'

'Perhaps you believe that, Mr George, but your actions don't suggest that. You intervened in an interaction between a young mother and her infant, verbally abusing the child and accusing the woman of being a bad parent. You admitted your actions to a policeman, and you've been found guilty of a breach of the peace. The facts are as stated, Mr George, and the court asked for a background report, which is why you and I are here. So far, you have shown no sign of contrition or regret for your behaviour.

You are an intelligent man, an unusual man, and you have overcome the difficulties of your childhood and early life. What can I say about you that might make the court look more leniently on you?'

That sounded to me like an eminently sensible opening, so I gave her my prepared speech.

'Dr Watson, I sincerely regret my behaviour, and I wish to apologise to the young woman, to her child, and to the police officer. I had been preoccupied in the week before the incident, since discovering the identity of my birth mother, and that she was still alive. That morning I had contacted her, and she had refused to meet me. She said her husband did not know of my existence, and she wanted to keep it that way, especially since I am of mixed race. She threatened me with violence from her brothers if I tried to make contact again. I knew that she had abandoned me when I was born, which is why I went into care. All this was going through my mind as I walked along Bath Street that day and saw the way this boy was behaving so disre-spectfully towards his mother. My feelings just burst to the surface and I could not stop myself from telling him what I thought of his behaviour. I am ashamed of myself, and I wish to assure you and the court that it will never happen again.'

'Thank you Mr George. I have recorded your statement and I will transcribe it as part of my report. I do hope I will not have to see you again in a professional capacity.'

'No, it is I who must thank you Dr Watson. I wonder … no, no, I shouldn't ask.'

'What, Mr George?'

'Well, please indulge me, Dr Watson. I have an interest

in studying forenames. If you don't mind, what does the L in your name stand for?'

'Lara, Mr George, it's Lara.'

How I resisted the urge to pump my fist in the air and shout 'YES' I do not know. I contented myself with a smile, a 'Thank you' and a shake of her hand. Right again, you sodding genius, right again.

~ Football crazy ~

Jᴇɴɴʏ ᴀʟᴡᴀʏs ᴍᴇᴀɴᴛ ᴡᴇʟʟ. It was such a shame things didn't always work out the way she hoped they would. But it never seemed to put her off trying to be helpful.

'Leave it Jenny. You can't help people who don't want to be helped.'

'But I'm sure if I could just tell Natalie what a pig her husband is ...'

'Don't go there Jenny. She knows he's a pig, but he's *her* pig.'

'How do you know?'

'I work with her. She's one of my team. She knows Jeremy's been unfaithful to her, but it's just the way he is. She's learned to live with it.'

'But don't you want her to be happy?'

'That's not part of my job description. I just need her to bring in more customers, and she does. She's very good at her job. That makes me happy and us a little bit richer.'

'Do you really mean that Tom? That's so heartless.'

'Come on, Jenny. I was being ironic.'

'Well, it sounded as if you meant it.'

The truth is, I'm every bit as sentimental as Jenny is, maybe even more so, but I keep it in check with a veneer of irony.

Some Sunday mornings our children are little angels, staying in their own rooms, keeping quiet, letting Mummy and Daddy stay in bed longer, to do whatever it is that mummies and daddies do in their beds, the thing that makes them happy and smiley all day long. This was not one of those Sundays. It seemed that I'd only just dozed off when little Annie appeared at the door, asking when breakfast would be ready. Brian wasn't far behind her, demanding to know what we would be doing that day.

Jenny groaned. 'Mum's been filling them up with sugar and nonsense again.'

'I think she does it to get even with you, for all the trouble you gave her as a teenager,' I said, but I was smiling. The fact is that I love my mother-in-law. Jean is a doting grandmother, but Jenny can't believe how well her mother and I get on together. The mother-in-law relationship isn't supposed to work like this. But she's a genuinely nice woman, and to me it's obvious where Jenny gets some of her best traits. She's easy to talk to, she's had an interesting life, including bringing up Jenny as a single mum, and she's got a very irreverent side to her character that I find extremely attractive. We're both inventively potty-mouthed on occasion, and Jenny raises her eyebrows in mock indignation. 'Honestly, you two!' she sighs, but she smiles as she says it.

Jenny was working a later shift, and I was on flexi, so it was my turn to pick up the kids. Annie's school was first, and then we had to wait for a half an hour before Brian's school finished. But she chattered away happily, I thought, and the time passed quickly. Brian dumped his bag in the boot, and came round to the front seat. I asked him how things had gone at the school. He muttered 'all right' in a manner which told me immediately it hadn't been 'all right', and I asked him to tell me what was wrong.

'Nothing's wrong, Dad. I was getting a bit of stick from one of the guys, but I sorted it.'

'Good, but next time let me know if I can help you sort things.'

'Of course. Can I ask you something Dad?'

'Yes?'

'What's the coolest musical instrument? To play, I mean.'

'Define cool,' I said.

'Well, everyone plays guitars, so they're not cool. Some play piano, but you can't carry one around, so they're not cool. There's brass band stuff, but you get lumpy lips with that, so they're not cool. So what else is there?'

'Saxophone. Girls love sax players, and that thing they do with their lips strengthens them, makes you a good kisser, so I'm told. Tenor sax is my favourite; it's deeper than alto, and you can play rock or jazz on it. Tenor players get the girls Brian.'

'That sounds cool.'

'I thought I knew where you were heading. I know how your mind works, young man.'

'You ever play sax, Dad?'

'No. I like to listen, but I never played. I did learn to kiss though.'

'Sheesh, Dad! You're gross' But Annie was laughing in the back seat.

'You want to learn saxophone?'

'Maybe when I go up to secondary. Only a year to go.'

'Saxophone's maybe a bit too big for you at the moment, Brian, but you could maybe start on a clarinet and move on to a saxophone when you're a bit older.' He looked pleased.

I served up the evening meal when Jenny came home

from work, and we had a lovely time together. Annie said, 'You're very pretty, Mummy.'

'Why thank you Annie. So are you.'

'Women!' said Brian, grinning at me.

'Oh yes, that reminds me,' I said. 'Brian and I were talking today, *mano a mano*,' I caught his smile. 'Anyway, he was telling me he's thinking about taking up a musical instrument in a couple of years. What do you think, Jenny?'

'That's an interesting idea. Maybe we could make the basement into a music room? It's not doing anything just now. Why don't we do it up as a playroom just now, and convert it later if either Brian or Annie get into music seriously?'

So over the next three weekends we decorated the big back room in the basement. It looked out into the back garden, so it was private. We hadn't really used it for much, and it still contained some of the junk we'd brought with us from our old house, five years before. We decided most of it really *was* junk, and I was delegated to take it down to our local recycling depot. Jenny sometimes calls me the resident Womble, because I try to recycle whatever's no longer needed. Then we moved a lot of the kids' toys from their rooms into the basement. Brian was grateful. We got him a desk for his bedroom so he could do his homework there. And we set up his speakers in the basement so he didn't disturb the rest of us listening to his music. Annie loved the playroom, and she turned her corner into a fantasyland, with Jenny helping her to hang drapes from the ceiling to screen 'her' domain off from the rest of the room.

It's funny: you know how girls are supposed to like the colour pink, cuddly toys and soft materials, only most of them don't? Annie did. She had a serious pink obsession.

Everything was pink. I thought it looked tacky, but of course I couldn't tell her that. She'd grow out of it, I thought. But she never did the tomboy stuff at all. She showed no interest in football, in climbing trees, fighting, or getting covered in mud, like most girls. She loved to dance, and she crooned the latest pop songs all the time—she knew all the words. She went off in a dream as she sang, totally into the words and the music. I thought she might turn out to be even more musical than her brother. They'd always been very fond of each other, didn't fight like most siblings, or not so often.

On Saturdays I was usually on football duty for Brian, taking him to and from local matches, if the school hadn't hired a minibus. But one Saturday in late October I had a cold and couldn't manage, so Jenny took him, while Annie stayed at home with me. They came back from the match very excited, and while Jenny left him in the bath to soak, she came in to see me.

'That was great fun Tom. I hadn't realised how exciting it could be, watching your son playing football. There were lots of other Mums there too, so I didn't feel conspicuous.'

I groaned. To be perfectly honest, I went with Brian out of a sense of fatherly duty. I actually can't stand sports of any kind, and standing freezing at the edge of a football pitch is not my favourite way to spend my scarce leisure hours. But I guess that's God's way of punishing fathers for having sex and producing sons.

'In America there's a name for people like you,' I said. 'Soccer Moms, they're called, spending their weekends ferrying their kids to and from sports.' I didn't tell her that fathers who transport their daughters to dance class are called Ballet Dads.

'I wouldn't mind becoming a Soccer Mom. It was great. Brian was man of the match. How about that then?'

'Not bad for an eleven-year old,' I said.

'It was at the end of the match that he clinched it. He and another boy ran up the pitch together, passing the ball between them to dodge the defenders. Then Jamie, the other boy, flicked the ball to Brian and he booted it straight in the net. I was so excited I grabbed the man standing next to me.'

'Wow, I bet most spectators don't get hugged at matches.'

'It turned out he's Jamie's dad.'

'Oh, Brian speaks about him, and I've met him at matches. He's bringing Jamie up on his own. Brian likes Jamie.'

'I asked them round for family tea on Monday. It would be good for both of them to get out more, I think.'

The tea went well. I liked Jamie's dad—Ken—and so did Jenny. It was always going to be Annie who asked, 'Where's Jamie's Mum?' Brian knew, of course, so he wouldn't have asked, and nor would Jenny.

'She lives in London now,' said Ken. 'Jamie sees her every month.'

I could see questions building up in Annie's head, so I changed the subject. When the kids went downstairs to the playroom, Ken gave us more details. He was surprisingly matter-of-fact and unemotional about the whole thing. I'm not sure if I'd have been able to talk about something like that in such a calm manner.

'Sandra met someone else, and we divorced. She's got two stepdaughters and a baby boy with her new man.'

'I'm sorry,' said Jenny. 'What about you?'

'I've had a couple of girlfriends, but nothing steady. I know Jamie would be more settled with female company around, but getting back in the dating scene is difficult at my age.'

I swear I could almost see a light bulb switching on above Jenny's head. This could be a new Project for her, no, a new *Mission*. I tried to deflect the subject.

'How's Jamie getting on at school?' I asked.

'Good actually. He works hard, he's a pretty serious boy. And he doesn't get into trouble. Your Brian helps a lot with that. They stick up for each other in the playground. The bullies leave them alone.'

I had suspected something like this might be going on at school, but Brian never spoke about it. He's a deep one, my son. Soon, all too soon, he and Jamie thundered back upstairs like a pair of casual rhinoceroses, and it was time for Ken to take Jamie home. In bed that night, Jenny started to talk about Ken, as I'd been certain she would.

'Ken's very nice,' she said.

'Yes. He seems a very good father to Jamie.'

'He does. He's sort of ... adjusted but unhappy, I'd say.'

'I think I know what you mean Jenny. But stick with the "adjusted" please. Don't get involved.'

'I won't get "involved" as you call it, but I was wondering if any of my single girlfriends might be interested.'

'I think that counts as "involved" Jenny. It's not a good idea.'

'If you say so, Tom. Goodnight,' she said, although I wasn't sure if she meant it. But the subject was closed for that night at least. Since the next day, Tuesday, was one of her working days, she turned over and switched off the light. She works a split-shift at the library, three days a week. She covers for lunch breaks, so most days she's able to get the kids off to school in the morning, and pick them up in the afternoon. She's gradually easing herself back into full-time work, which she'll probably start when Annie's in the upper primary and Brian is in secondary. Her colleagues like her, and she gets on well with the public. Nominally I work flexi-hours, so I can cover school run duties if she can't manage it. In practice, I work well over my allotted hours, like most people in this wretched economy. I'm in sales, so I'm often running hard just to stand still.

My Tuesday started at 8.30 as usual, but it didn't usually start with a visit from the boss of bosses, Sir Andrew himself, with a cohort of yes-people, some of whom were clearly still rubbing the sleep from their eyes.

'Good morning Simpson,' he said, checking the nameplate on my desk. 'Congratulations on your team's performance last year. You brought in 5% more business last year, when the rest of Sales were down 2. I'm calling a meeting of the heads of all the Sales teams in Head Office next month, and I want you to talk to them, tell them how you did it. We'll put you and one of your team up in a nice hotel, and give you an allowance. What do you say?'

What else could I say but 'Of course, Sir Andrew.'

They left, after much hand-shaking from people I'd heard of vaguely, and others I'd never heard of at all. Then I sought out Natalie. Of course I picked Natalie to come with me. And she was delighted, to the extent of a squeal and a hug, both of which I enjoyed.

Jenny was on duty that day, so I couldn't talk to her directly to give her the good news, but I had left her a short triumphalist message, and said I'd be late home. Natalie and I worked on the presentation we would deliver in London. We would concentrate on our strong points, our strategies and our sales scripts, since we'd gone off-message and developed our own ways of working. I figured my team would score big Brownie Points from this if management adopted our methods, and the company would benefit, and hence we would too, in a sort of virtuous circle.

I was fairly tired when I got home, and the kids were already in bed. Annie was asleep, but I had the chance to annoy Brian by tousling his hair. Allow me a little bit of fatherly mischief please; it's fun to irritate your children. I re-heated a bit of supper in the microwave, and went upstairs for an early night. And then Jenny came to bed.

'I've been thinking, Tom.'

'Oh no,' I groaned.

'I was wondering about Geraldine—for Ken I mean.'

'Geraldine? She's the least stable of your friends. Do you want to drive him nuts?'

'She's not unstable. Maybe a bit neurotic, but she's very nice. And she's extremely attractive.'

'So why didn't her marriage last? Why is she still single five years after the divorce?'

'It wasn't her fault. He took a mistress.'

'What I heard it was just an impulse thing, a one-night stand.'

'Well, whatever. He was definitely unfaithful.'

'He told me he discovered she'd had a whole series of affairs.'

'They weren't affairs, they were just romantic friendships, Tom. Anyway, I've given her Ken's number, they can take it from there.'

That Saturday Brian and Jamie were playing again, and

Jenny said she'd take Brian and bring Jamie back with us for a sleepover, as Ken had a date.

'With Geraldine?' I asked, already sure of the answer.

Geraldine phoned Jenny on the Sunday to say they'd a had a wonderful time on Saturday night, a nice meal, a few drinks, and back to Ken's place for coffee and chat. She was sure he would phone her during the week and make another date. 'See,' said Jenny. 'I told you it would work out.'

'Don't count your chickens before the horse has bolted,' I said.

Jenny and Geraldine exchanged phone calls every night that week. Ken hadn't phoned Geraldine back, and she was becoming increasingly unhappy. Jenny told me she would phone Ken, and I vetoed that idea straight away. 'That would constitute interference, Jenny. You mustn't do it.' And I think she reluctantly agreed it would be. On the following Saturday I said I'd take Brian to the school playing fields, since Jenny had taken him to the last three matches. Ken was there of course. He seemed slightly disappointed to see me.

'Jenny not here today? Is she all right?'

'Fine,' I said. 'She's taking Annie shopping today.'

'I just wondered,' he said.

'Look Ken, tell me it's none of my business and I'll shut up, but I know Jenny was trying to set you up with her friend Geraldine last weekend, and Geraldine's been phoning every night since. Do you want to talk about it?'

'It was a disaster, Tom. I mean she looks really nice, but I couldn't hold a conversation with her. She was just so over-eager it turned me off. She wasn't interested in listening to me. She kept asking me questions and then answering them herself, *and* she got most of the answers wrong.

Then, back at the flat she just threw herself at me and tried to kiss me. I'm afraid I got angry, but I tried not to show it. I just said it was too soon for me and we should call it a night, and I phoned for a taxi.'

'I was afraid it would go wrong. I've known Geraldine for ages, and that doesn't surprise me at all.'

'I hate being rushed into things, Tom. Oh, well done Brian,' he shouted, and we both clapped. 'I'm not looking for a passionate sexual relationship. Frankly Tom, I'd rather have a cuddle. But I'm looking for somebody who'd be good with Jamie. He's a super lad. He knows he won't get his Mum back, but he needs an adult female in his life, as much as I do. Do me a favour Tom?'

'Of course. What do you want?'

'Thank Jenny for me, but please tell her not to try matchmaking for me. I will find someone eventually, but it'll be my way.'

'That's what I'm always trying to tell her. She's very well-meaning, but she doesn't always put herself in the other person's shoes. She thinks she knows best what's good for other people.'

'She should be a politician.'

'God forbid, Ken. Getting colder, isn't it?'

'Shouldn't be surprised if it rains.'

'Tom.'

'Yes Ken?'

'Please don't be too hard on Jenny. I don't want her to get upset over this.'

'Of course. Would you do something for her please?' He nodded. 'Phone Geraldine and let her down gently. Could you do that?'

'Certainly. I've been feeling guilty about it, to be honest.

I'll just tell her we're not right for each other, which is true, and that I wish her well, which is also true. I've never had to do this before, or not since before Sandra and I got together, which feels like forever ago.'

The match was coming to an end, in a one all draw, which was about right, I thought, and then in injury time Jamie came round the outside, near the corner post, jinked past two defenders, and shot a tremendous cross which swerved inside the goalkeeper and pitched into the net. The boys jumped in the air as the final whistle blew, and Ken and I did a little dance on the side-line. Result!

I drove home with Brian, working on a sales pitch I could use on Jenny. She'd be uncomfortable. Damn it, *I* was uncomfortable, and it was her fault.

'Right, filthy Brian, upstairs and into the bath. Leave your muddy strip on the floor, and I'll take it down to the utility room. You can clean up your boots tomorrow.'

'Thanks Dad,' he said. 'We were good, weren't we?'

'You were, and Jamie is a star.'

'He definitely is. That goal was *A. Maze. Ing.*'

'Certainly was. Get clean and change for your meal.'

I strolled into the kitchen. 'Did Ken say anything about Geraldine?' Jenny asked.

'A bit. We'll talk about it when the kids are down,' I said.

Over supper I told the story of the match, and all about Jamie's brilliant goal. Jenny teased me about me becoming a sports commentator, and I said I'd have to polish up my clichés. Later, Jenny came downstairs after settling the kids in bed. I was watching the repeat of an Attenborough wildlife thing on the box, and I switched it off.

'So,' said Jenny. 'Ken and Geraldine.'

'Yes,' I said. 'Ken said to thank you for trying to help him, but he asks you, in the nicest possible way, to let him do it his way in future.'

'Oh no. Did he say what went wrong with Geraldine?'

'Yes. He said she was very attractive, but she was a bit too eager for his liking, and he didn't think she'd be right for Jamie. I said he should phone her and tell her.'

'Thanks Tom. I'll apologise to him too. I'll phone him tomorrow. I just hoped they might hit it off.'

'Don't forget I'm off to London tomorrow afternoon.'

'Do you want a lift to the station?'

'No, it's all right. I'll get the Metro. I'm meeting Natalie at 2. I'm not sure which train we'll catch on Monday— some time in the afternoon. I'll text you.'

'What time's your presentation?'

'Nine-thirty, then we've got Q&As and discussions, so it'll take up most of the morning. I'm having an early night, pet.' So I kissed her goodnight and went to bed.

Natalie was at Newcastle Central when I arrived, looking attractive but very professional. The company had paid for first class travel, and we enjoyed that. I used to be excited when I had trips to London in the early days, visiting all the museums and famous landmarks, but now I can't be bothered with the place. There's really nothing here that I want; Newcastle feels much more friendly, and I like my little part of it. We got to our hotel and checked in, then arranged to meet in the business centre with our laptops, to go over our presentation, and to try to anticipate questions. I like to be well prepared, and so does Natalie.

In the evening, we walked out of the hotel and spotted a

Vietnamese restaurant. I like the food, but Natalie hadn't eaten in one before.

'Is it like Thai food?' she asked.

'A bit, but it's really unique. There's a choice in this one; you can have a starter and one of the main courses, or you can ask for a selection of Vietnamese street food.'

I had the Pho Bo, a rich and spicy beef-based soup which was a meal in itself, while Natalie tried the street food selection.

'I'm converted Tom. That was delicious. I wonder if there's a Vietnamese restaurant at home?'

'Two or three. I'll treat you when we get back.'

'Are you nervous about tomorrow, Tom?'

'No. You?'

She shook her head. 'We're well prepared. Your handouts are good.'

We wandered back to the hotel and I suggested a drink in the bar. 'We should probably just have one drink, Natalie, just to settle ourselves.'

Next morning we took a cab to Head Office, and got the technology connected up. Then the sales teams filed in, and the Sales Director, Dr Bridgeman, introduced us. Sir Andrew was sitting beside him, so that set the tone for the meeting—professional, high-powered, serious, respectful. Natalie and I were so well rehearsed that our actual pitch was very smooth. Then the questions started, and we answered them well and with confidence. Sir Andrew stood up and thanked us, saying he was convinced that the other sales teams should learn from our success. If that wasn't a steer then I don't know what is. Then he headed off somewhere, leaving us with Dr Bridgeman. He came straight to the point.

'I like your ideas, and I want you to work on putting some of them into a new sales manual. Would you be happy with that Tom?'

'I would Sir, but can I suggest Natalie takes the lead for me in this? I know she can do it, and I'd like to give her the chance to work at a higher level.' Natalie was surprised by this—we hadn't talked about it—but she kept her cool and said she'd be delighted. And that was that. A considerable success for both of us. Mine would be reflected in my bonuses, and Natalie's in a promotion. And I'd still be leading my team, although I thought we'd probably expand it a bit now. Neither of us wanted to hang around, so we headed off to King's Cross for our train home. I texted Jenny to say it had gone well, and we were homeward bound. She replied <*Great. See you soon. Geraldine phoned. Going round to her place after supper.*>

I must admit I'd forgotten about the Ken and Geraldine situation, but I assumed things had been more or less settled. When we were seated in our carriage, Natalie said, 'Thanks for saying what you did Tom. You have no idea how good that made me feel. And it's given me the confidence to decide to move on with my life. I've made up my mind I'm going to divorce Jeremy.'

'Gosh. Big changes Natalie, but I know you'll make it. And you're still part of the team. You know we can talk about anything.'

Jenny had picked up the children by the time I got home, and we had a nice little celebratory meal, with white wine for Jenny and I, and Pepsi as a treat for the kids. Then Jenny bustled about, getting ready for her night out with Geraldine. 'Just a few drinks and a chat, Tom. I won't be late.' The taxi arrived and she was off. I gave Annie her bath—

177

Brian thinks he's too grown-up for me to bath him—got them settled in to bed. I had a second glass of wine, feeling very relaxed.

When Jenny came in she didn't say much about Geraldine, just that Ken had phoned her, and she had accepted the situation. On the Wednesday she said she was going out to the pub with Geraldine for an hour or so. Again, she didn't say much when she got home, but she said that Brian was going to stay over at Jamie's after the match on Saturday, and Ken wanted her to join them for a little meal that night to show off his cooking skills.

After Annie was down on the Saturday I got absorbed in a TV football match, of all things, and I didn't notice how much time had passed until I heard Jenny's car in the driveway. I looked at my watch—10:30—thinking that was rather late to come home after a post-match meal with Ken and the boys. I waited for her to come in, but after five minutes there was no sign of her, so I opened the door and walked round to the car. Jenny was still in the driving seat, face down over the steering wheel, arms around her head. Getting closer, I heard her sobbing.

Acknowledgements

The Literary Consultancy, specifically Natalie Galustian, gave very helpful editorial comments on the original draft manuscript. I'm also grateful to friends who have read and commented on individual stories.

A NOTE ON THE TYPE

The text of this book is set in Miller, designed
by Matthew Carter and released in 1997.
It is a 'Scotch Roman', and follows the original style in
having both roman and italic small capitals. The style
was developed from types cut by Richard Austin
between 1810 and 1820 at the Edinburgh
type foundries of Alexander Wilson and William Miller.